What Reviewers Say About Bold Strokes Books

"With its expected unexpected twists, vivid characters and healthy dose of humor, *Blind Curves* is a very fun read that will keep you guessing."—*Bay Windows*

"In a succinct film style narrative, with scenes that move, a character-driven plot, and crisp dialogue worthy of a screenplay…the Richfield and Rivers novels are…an engaging Hollywood mystery…series."—*Midwest Book Review*

Force of Nature "…is filled with nonstop, fast paced action. Tornadoes, raging fire blazes, heroic and daring rescues…Baldwin does a fine job of describing the fast-paced scenes and inspiring the reader to keep on turning the pages."—*L-word.com Literature*

In the Jude Devine mystery series the "…characters seem fully capable of walking away from the particulars of whodunit and engaging the reader in other aspects of their lives."—*Lambda Book Report*

Mine "…weaves a tale of yearning, love, lust, and conflict resolution…a believable plot, with strong characters in a charming setting." – *Just About Write*

"While these two women struggle with their issues, there is some very, very hot sex. If you enjoy complex characters and passionate sex scenes, you'll love *Wild Abandon*."—*MegaScene*

"*Course of Action* is a romance…populated with a host of captivating and amiable characters. The glimpses into the lifestyles of the rich and beautiful people are rather like guilty pleasures…a most satisfying and entertaining reading experience."—*Midwest Book Review*

The Clinic is "…a spellbinding novel."—*Just About Write*

"*Unexpected Sparks* lived up to its promise and was thoroughly enjoyable…Dartt did a lovely job at building the relationship between Kate and Nikki."—*Lambda Book Report*

"*Sequestered Hearts*…is everything a romance should be. It is teeming with longing, heartbreak, and of course, love. As pure romances go, it is one of the best in print today."—*L-word.com Literature*

"*The Exile and the Sorcerer* is a mesmerizing read, a tour-de-force packed with adventure, ordeals, complex twists and turns, and the internal introspection of appealing characters."—*Midwest Book Review*

The Spanish Pearl is "…both science fiction and romance in this adventurous tale…A most entertaining read, with a sequel already in the works. Hot, hot, hot!"—*Minnesota Literature*

"A deliciously sexy thriller...*Dark Valentine* is funny, scary, and very realistic. The story is tightly written and keeps the reader gripped to the exciting end."—*Just About Write*

"*Punk Like Me*...is different. It is engaging. It is life-affirming. Frankly, it is genius. This is a rare book in that it has a soul; one that is laid bare for all to see."—*Just About Write*

"*Chance* is not a novel about the music industry; it is about a woman discovering herself as she muddles through all the trappings of fame."—*Midwest Book Review*

Sweet Creek "...is sublimely in tune with the times."—*Q-Syndicate*

"*Forever Found*...neatly combines hot sex scenes, humor, engaging characters, and an exciting story."—*MegaScene*

Shield of Justice is a "...well-plotted...lovely romance...I couldn't turn the pages fast enough!"—Ann Bannon, author of *The Beebo Brinker Chronicles*

The 100th Generation is "...filled with ancient myths, Egyptian gods and goddesses, legends, and, most wonderfully, it contains the lesbian equivalent of Indiana Jones living and working in modern Egypt."—*Just About Write*

Sword of the Guardian is "...a terrific adventure, coming of age story, a romance, and tale of courtly intrigue, attempted assassination, and gender confusion...a rollicking fun book and a must-read for those who enjoy courtly light fantasy in a medieval-seeming time."—*Midwest Book Review*

"*Of Drag Kings and the Wheel of Fate*'s lush rush of a romance incorporates reincarnation, a grounded transman and his peppy daughter, and the dark moods of a troubled witch—wonderful homage to Leslie Feinberg's classic gender-bending novel, *Stone Butch Blues*."—*Q-Syndicate*

In *Running with the Wind* "...the discussions of the nature of sex, love, power, and sexuality are insightful and represent a welcome voice from the view of late-20-something characters today."—*Midwest Book Review*

"Rich in character portrayal, *The Devil Inside* is an unusual, unpredictable, and thought-provoking love story that will have the reader questioning the definition of right and wrong long after she finishes the book."—*Just About Write*

Wall of Silence "...is perfectly plotted and has a very real voice and consistently accurate tone, which is not always the case with lesbian mysteries."—*Midwest Book Review*

05/19

WITHDRAWN

Visit us at www.boldstrokesbooks.com

AWAKENING TO SUNLIGHT

by

Lindsey Stone

A Division of Bold Strokes Books

2010

AWAKENING TO SUNLIGHT

ISBN 10: 1-60282-143-7
ISBN 13: 978-1-60282-143-9

This Trade Paperback Original Is Published By
Bold Strokes Books, Inc.
P.O. Box 249
Valley Falls, NY 12185

First Edition: March 2010

Credits
Editors: Cindy Cresap and Stacia Seaman
Production Design: Stacia Seaman
Cover Design By Sheri (graphicartist2020@hotmail.com)

Acknowledgments

A thank you note to:

My mother for introducing me to the magic of books at such an early age and for planting within me the seeds of compassion and understanding.

&

The children's authors who helped mould my imagination and to all the authors that followed; from the classics to the contemporary. Your works have been inspiring.

&

Aline, for believing in me and supporting me in my endeavours.

&

Mama Tijger, for your enthusiasm

&

Cindy Cresap, my editor, for pointing out all those annoying distancing POVs.

&

Stacia Seaman, my copy editor, for the final tweaking.

&

To my loyal shadow; my stubborn, but cuddly Belgium Shepherd dog for putting up with my through-the-night writing, when all she wanted to do was go to bed.

&

Finally, but not least, to Len Barot and her amazing team. Bold Strokes Books has managed to raise the bar, and the literary world is the better for it.

Dedication

With our eyes open
Over the hurdles of life
In the wake of pain
In search of meaning
All which prove we are alive

There are those that fall
Those that carry on
And those who come to realise the importance of love

I dedicate this book to you

The Shadow on the Stone

I went by the Druid stone
That broods in the garden white and lone,
And I stopped and looked at the shifting shadows
That at some moments fall thereon
From the tree hard by with a rhythmic swing,
And they shaped in my imagining
To the shade that a well-known head and shoulders
Threw there when she was gardening.

I thought her behind my back,
Yea, her I long had learned to lack,
And I said: 'I am sure you are standing behind me,
Though how do you get into this old track?'
And there was no sound but the fall of a leaf
As a sad response; and to keep down grief
I would not turn my head to discover
That there was nothing in my belief.

Yet I wanted to look and see
That nobody stood at the back of me;
But I thought once more: 'Nay, I'll not unvision
A shape which, somehow, there may be.'
So I went on softly from the glade,
And left her behind me throwing her shade,
As she were indeed an apparition—
My head unturned lest my dream should fade.

—Thomas Hardy

PROLOGUE

Lizzy's heart raced and it seemed to pause every few seconds, causing the muscles in her chest to contract, but she dug her clammy fists even deeper into her pockets and concentrated on walking down the gray-floored corridor.

When she'd first made her way down this corridor, just a few months ago, she had recognized the interior designer's attempt at making the place seem friendlier and less daunting by hanging colorful pictures along the pastel walls. She had initially appreciated the improvement of man's sensitivity since medieval times and yet it had still felt patronizing to her, somehow. As if cheerful surroundings were in some way supposed to make things better. Then, as pain and despair became the constant thread of each day and hope quickly faded away, she had come to resent the implication. Now, as she headed down the familiar corridor for the zillionth time, all that she could see were her feet and the space they would soon no longer take up.

Her whole body burned with fear for what she knew to be true, but would not, could not accept. She'd been asked not to come until the evening, and while others had been called for throughout the day, she had had to wait patiently, enduring long, agonizing hours for the moment she feared most. As she placed her hand on the doorknob she paused; her chest felt like it was slowly tearing open. She tried to muster up a smile, but the contradiction was too much for her tormented mind to cope with. She took a deep breath, prayed for strength, and opened the door.

After all the pain and the bombardment of deadly foreign toxins, her lover's weakened body had withered to no more than a shadow of its former self, but to Lizzy she was still beautiful and her heart seemed to calm a little at merely being in the same room as her. For the first time in months Maurice's body was free from the web of sterile tubes and wiring that had helped keep her prisoner to the bed. Even the monitor that had stood next to the bed for endless days and nights diligently recording the ebbing pulses of her life was now dormant. Only one line of tubing remained for the morphine, the only thing that had been of any help. She didn't dare move as she listened to the only sound that filled the deafening silence of the room, Maurice's shallow, labored breathing. Lizzy wished with all her heart that she could just wrap her up in her arms and take her home. All she wanted was to hold her and never have to let go. Maurice stirred and slowly opened her eyes.

"Is that you, dear?"

Maurice's voice was so coarse and weak that it tore at her heart, but she did her utmost to try to sound lighthearted. "Yes, gorgeous, it's me." She walked over to the bed and gently kissed her on the forehead. "I missed you today."

"I missed you too."

Lizzy reached for a chair and pulled it up close to the bed and gently took hold of Maurice's pale hand. It felt cold and she cupped it tighter, willing the warmth back.

"How's the pain today?"

"Not as bad as it normally is."

Lizzy managed a weak smile. "That's good."

She felt so lame, so goddamned useless, and she searched for words that would somehow make a difference.

Maurice slowly lifted her arm and gently stroked the side of her head.

"We need to talk."

Lizzy didn't want to listen, she didn't want to hear the words, she just wanted to feel Maurice's touch.

"It's time, sweet pea. I can feel it."

Lizzy fought hard against the tears intent on falling and struggled to keep the anger she felt at bay.

"I can't. I can't do this."

"Yes, you can. You have to."

Maurice's words made no sense in Lizzy's universe and all she could do was shake her head in response.

"You have to promise me something, sweet pea. I want you to live your life for the both of us. I want you to keep your heart open…" She paused and inhaled a long, labored breath. "Don't be scared to love again."

The words were beyond Lizzy's comprehension and yet she knew that these painful words were bravely spoken, meant as a precious gift in a final act of selfless love, but she didn't want them. The mere fact that Maurice could even think that someone else would ever be able to take her place or that she could ever want anybody else tore into the very depths of her soul. The tears she had tried so hard to hold back rolled down her cheeks and anger pulsated through her veins.

"Please, please, don't do this, I can't do this."

"Listen to me, Lizzy. You were the best thing that ever happened to me. I consider myself extremely lucky. I've had love in my life, I've had you. I've made peace with my fate and you have to do the same."

Lizzy could hardly breathe, her insides were so constricted that her words came out as mere whispers between her tears. "My life means nothing without you."

"Yes, it does. Your life had meaning before we met and now you have to find a new meaning to it. I have loved you with all my heart and I ask this last thing of you. Promise me, Lizzy, promise me, please."

What she was asking was unbearable, but so too was the anguish in Maurice's fragile voice, and so Lizzy dug deep inside her soul to find the strength to give her what she wanted. "I...I promise."

Maurice's eyelids fluttered and she sighed. "I can feel it, Lizzy, I can feel the peace spreading through my body."

The lines of pain that had cast shadows upon Maurice's delicate features turned soft with tranquility.

"Kiss me one more time, Lizzy, for the journey."

Wordlessly, Lizzy leaned forward and gently kissed the only woman she had ever loved. Maurice made the familiar soft sound she often made when they kissed in private and the warm air of her breath caressed Lizzy's skin as it passed between them. Then she felt Maurice's lips relax and her hand slowly slip off her back. At that moment she felt oblivion take hold of her, and as her chest ripped open, her mind exploded into nothingness. The whole world stopped dead in its tracks and all that breathed was the black hole inside her chest.

Chapter One

Judith stood in front of her wardrobe frantically trying to decide what to take. She knew she couldn't take everything, but couldn't make up her mind what would be the most sensible. The doorbell rang and she dashed out of the bedroom, nearly tripping over a pair of shoes she had only moments before set aside ready to pack. Chris looked immaculate as ever in his suit and tie, but it was clear he was feeling very uncomfortable standing on her doorstep. She hadn't known him for long, but there hadn't been anyone else she could turn to and when she'd called him earlier in desperation to ask for his help, he hadn't hesitated. He'd promised to leave work and come for her as soon as possible, and he had. She stepped aside to let him in.

"Thanks for doing this. You have no idea how grateful I am."

"No problem." He stepped into the hall and nervously glanced around. "I take it he isn't back yet?"

"No."

Chris's shoulders seemed to relax a little. "I think we'd better get a move on and avoid any chance of a confrontation."

"I'm nearly ready, but I'm finding it difficult deciding what to take."

"Just try to think practical."

Judith pulled a face. "That's what I've been trying to do."

"Is there anything I can take out to the car already?"

"Well, Emily's things are already packed. There's this bag

here," She pointed to a children's backpack resting against the wall on her left. "And the rest is in her bedroom, the second door on the right."

"Okay. I'll take them out to the car while you finish up."

Judith rushed back to her own bedroom repeating Chris's words to herself. *Think practical.* She walked over to her underwear cabinet and scooped out whatever her hands landed on, then threw the pile of clothes into the suitcase that lay open on her bed. She then turned back to her wardrobe and frantically grabbed two of everything off the hangers and threw them in as well. Her once neatly ironed and folded clothes now lay in a jumbled heap in her suitcase. She grabbed the book she'd been reading from the nightstand and threw it on top, pulled the lid down, and with somewhat of a struggle, zipped it shut. She took a step back and blew a strand of hair off her face and wondered if there was anything else she would need. She stared at her neatly made-up double bed with her bulging suitcase on top and a question thundered through her mind: *What on earth am I doing?*

Chris appeared at the doorway. "Are you ready?"

Judith didn't turn to face him, but instead picked up the framed photo she had kept on her dresser, a snapshot of what once had been better times.

"Am I being an idiot?"

Chris didn't hesitate. "No. You're doing the right thing."

"You really think so?"

"Absolutely."

"You don't think I'm overreacting?"

"I think you should have left the jerk years ago."

Judith plopped herself onto the bed and rested her pounding head in her hands.

"But it seems so final, so sudden, and so drastic!"

Chris entered the room and knelt in front of her.

"It's not sudden, though, is it, Judith? Things have been building up for a long time now and maybe it is final, I don't know, maybe it's not. Maybe when he comes home and finds you gone he'll sit down and realize what an ass he's been. Either way, you need to get out of here for a while, if only to get things straight in your own head."

She knew Chris was right. Things hadn't been right for a long time and she did need time to think and get her thoughts straight, but she was scared. Deep down she knew her life was about to change in a big way. She just didn't know if she could handle it. She felt weak and a failure. Wasn't she just running away from her problems instead of trying to solve them? Had she tried hard enough?

Chris took her hands in his. "Judith, I know it's hard, but you know that this is the right thing to do and not just for yourself, but for Emily too. Now I do think we should get going. He could turn up at any moment." Chris stood again and reached for the suitcase. "I'll meet you out at the car."

Judith chewed the inside of her mouth as she watched him lift the bloated suitcase off the bed and stagger with it out of the room. Then she took a deep breath and surveyed her bedroom one last time. It was all so quiet and surreal. She knew she should be doing something like peeling the potatoes for dinner or doing some washing, but instead she was in the process of walking out on her life as she knew it. She thought back to yesterday and how she had felt when Menno had arrived home from work. Like every other day, she had grown anxious as the hour drew nearer for his return, and like every other day, she had not known whether he was going to come home indifferent or angry. Regardless, she knew there was going to be something she hadn't done right to set him off on one of his relentless, belittling monologues.

Yesterday, though, something had changed. She couldn't remember what it was he had been accusing her of, but instead of crumbling at his words she had felt an unexpected calmness and had known at that moment, she had to leave. She didn't quite understand it, but just thinking it had made it the only way forward and now she was going to have to be strong, for herself and for Emily. *Emily!* She checked her watch. It was a quarter to four. Without a second glance she raced out of the bedroom, down the hall, grabbing her coat from the coat rack on the way, and opened the door to the outside world.

As she pulled the front door shut she quietly prayed: *Dear God, please let me be doing the right thing!*

Fifteen minutes later they were waiting outside Emily's school. Judith was trying to think of a way to explain it all to Emily without hurting or confusing her, but it seemed impossible to explain something that she herself didn't yet understand. She looked out the car window at all the other parents waiting and wondered what they would say if they were her.

"I'm sorry you can't stay with us. It's just that we do this every year. Tom's family flies over here from Australia and stays at our place while we fly over there and stay at theirs. Otherwise it wouldn't have been a problem."

Judith turned to face him and tapped his leg, appreciating his concern.

"Don't be silly, you don't have to apologize. You're doing more than enough already."

"You'll like it at Lizzy's anyway. The apartment has got lots of original features in it and it has a roof terrace."

"I haven't even asked you where it is exactly."

"It's on the west side of town. Marnixkade."

"And you're sure she's okay with this? I know I wouldn't like the idea of having strangers stay in my home."

"Lizzy's cool. She won't mind."

Judith turned to look out the window again when it dawned on her what Chris had just said. In shock she turned back to face him.

"You made that sound as if she doesn't know yet!"

Chris winced. "Well, she doesn't."

"Chris!" Judith's anxiety turned to panic.

"Calm down. I tried to call her, but I kept getting her voicemail."

"So she hasn't given her consent and doesn't even know we're coming?"

Chris winced a little at Judith's question. "No, not yet, but—"

"Oh God, Chris, you said it was okay!"

"It is okay. I promise you, Lizzy won't mind."

"How can you be sure if you haven't spoken to her? I can't just camp out in someone's home without their consent!"

"Trust me! I've known Lizzy since we were kids. It won't be a problem."

Judith spotted Emily coming through the school doors surrounded by other energetic seven-year-olds and knew she had no choice now but to trust that Chris was right. She got out of the car and waved to Emily, who excitedly waved back as she came running full speed toward her. Judith knelt and caught her in her arms and gave her a big hug.

"Mommy, guess what we've being painting today?"

"What's that, sweetheart?"

"Our own faces." Emily's beaming smile soothed away some of the panic Judith was feeling.

"Wow, that must have been hard."

"It was, because we had to do it from memory, but Lisa pretended to go to the bathroom so she could look in the mirror."

"Did she now?"

Emily leaned to one side to get a better look at the car parked behind Judith.

"Whose car is that, Mommy?"

"It belongs to a friend of mine. His name is Chris and he's going to give us a lift."

"How come?"

"Well…" Judith hesitated and tried to continue in a casual tone. "You and I are going to be staying somewhere for a few days and Chris is here to help us with our bags."

Emily took on that familiar frown she always made when she was trying to work something out.

"Is Daddy coming?"

Her words pierced like a knife. How many times had she witnessed Emily's hurt and her sadness as he rejected her time and time again, and how hard had Emily tried to win his love and attention only to be shunned and pushed away?

Judith tried hard to hold back the tears that welled up. She loved her daughter so much and all she wanted to do was to protect her. "No, darling, Daddy's not coming. It will just be you and me."

Emily stared into her eyes and Judith held her breath. She desperately wanted to say something reassuring and to give her the explanation she was owed, but then, to her relief, Emily's frown disappeared and she simply accepted it with an even, "Okay, Mommy."

Judith felt too choked with emotion to speak, but pulled Emily in close again, hugging her tightly, and silently promised she would do whatever it took to make things right.

Chris weaved his way across town through the hordes of meandering tourists, tooting cars, and local Amsterdamers peddling with death-defying expertise in between and around everything in their path, before finally turning off into a quiet narrow side street. It was a charming street typical of Amsterdam. It was lined on either side with tall traditional narrow seventeenth-century houses all boasting elaborate decorative stone gables, revealing the occupations of the industrious trading merchants who once owned them. A quiet narrow canal, lined with lush green trees, ran down the middle of the street, separating one side from the other. At each end was a low wooden bridge with black decorative railings stretching across the canal, enhancing the quaintness and overall tranquility of the street.

Like everywhere else in Amsterdam, all the parking spaces were filled with cars that never seemed to move, but Chris spotted a small space at the end of the street and decided to try to squeeze the car into it. Parking in Amsterdam was not for the faint-hearted. People often drove their cars into the canal while trying to park, and Judith held her breath while Chris carefully maneuvered the car until he finally managed to squeeze it in, albeit at a weird angle.

Chris finally pulled up the hand brake and sighed victoriously before speaking. "It's only four doors back." He turned off the ignition and turned to her with a slight grimace. "I have to warn you, though, it's also four flights of stairs we have to climb."

Some minutes later they all stood on a small landing panting and sweating. Chris plonked the bulging suitcase on the ground.

"I have to do something about my condition."

Judith dropped the sport bags she was carrying. "That makes two of us."

"It's harder for me because I have shorter legs," Emily quipped.

Both Chris and Judith burst out laughing at Emily's statement. Then Chris dug out the keys, unlocked the front door, and led them inside.

Judith was certainly impressed. The apartment was surprisingly spacious without being cavernous, and she especially liked the living room. Tall wall-to-wall windows allowed an extraordinary array of light to penetrate and fill every corner of the room. The walls were painted a soft cream color that contrasted beautifully with the warm oak floor. In the center were three big, comfortable-looking couches deliberately placed around a welcoming authentic fireplace. At the far end of the living room was an open kitchen, and off to the side was an alcove that functioned as an adequate dining area. The whole setting was simplistically elegant, yet cozy and warm. They followed Chris around as he showed them the rest of the apartment, which Judith found to be tastefully decorated. He pointed out Lizzy's bedroom and study without entering before finally showing them the two guest rooms they could use.

"This place is great."

"I knew you'd like it." Chris smiled knowingly.

"It must have cost a ton!"

"Well, the place was in a pretty bad shape when she bought it, so she got it for a good price and she did most of the work on it herself. Come on, there's one more thing I want you to see."

Chris led them back down the hall and through the living room and opened the two bay doors leading out onto the roof terrace. Chris had been right; it was gorgeous. It was like a private oasis hidden in between the rooftops. The terrace was built of wood and was about six yards by six yards. It had a garden table and chairs tucked away to the left and lots of plant pots and hanging baskets all around. Although there were no flowers in them, Judith could easily imagine how beautiful it could be. The terrace owed its privacy to the surrounding rooftops, but ahead the view was clear and Judith could see quite far into the city's center.

"Chris, this is lovely. It's like a secret hideaway from the world."

"I knew you'd like it. Everybody does. Look, I have to get going if I'm going to finish my packing on time."

Judith accompanied him back to the front door listening to further information, like where to find the clean linens and such.

"Oh, I nearly forgot." He took out his bunch of keys, unhooked two, and passed them to her explaining that one was for this door and one was for the downstairs door. Judith accepted the keys and studied them resting in her palm. Her earlier apprehension rushed back.

"Chris, I really don't feel comfortable staying in this woman's house without her permission."

"Judith, you must believe me, Lizzy won't mind, and besides, she won't be back for another three weeks."

"But still, I—"

"If it makes you feel better, then I promise to keep calling her."

Judith nodded taking some comfort from that. "Thank you, Chris, for everything you've done for us today."

"No problem. I'll try to call you in a few days, to see how you're doing."

"No, don't. I don't want you thinking about me while you're on vacation. I'll call you when you get back and let you know where I am."

"Are you sure?"

"Yes. Don't worry. I'll be fine. You just go and enjoy yourself. I'll see you when you get back."

Chris gave her a hug, wished her luck, and then left. As she listened to his footsteps disappear down the stairs, she wondered what on earth she was supposed to do next. She headed back to the living room and watched Emily playing on the terrace.

She felt completely out of place and utterly alone.

Chapter Two

Lizzy closed the door behind her with a deep sigh and leaned against it feeling utterly frustrated with herself for being so stupid. After a few moments of chastising herself she walked over to the bed and with a feeling of total exasperation, let herself fall back onto it. She thought back to when Kees Dekker, the big-time producer, had approached her. He'd called her out of the blue, explaining how impressed he'd been with her latest movie and that he had something she might be interested in. At first she'd tactfully tried to put him off, telling him she was grateful for the offer but was smack-bang in the middle of preproduction for a new movie already and had neither the time nor the funding to get distracted. She hadn't lied, but she had withheld her real reason for turning it down—she didn't like mainstream moviemaking and had once vowed never to go down that road. Kees Dekker was renowned for his tenacity, and he had been persistent in his conviction that she would find it worth her while and insisted she at least read the script before turning the project down. She'd finally agreed to read it on the premise that he would leave her alone if she still wasn't interested.

The following morning the script had arrived by courier and she'd reluctantly sat to read it. She'd stopped only once for a bathroom break and a fresh cup of tea, pausing every once in a while to jot down thoughts on camera positions and the like. Kees had been right. The script was good, and there was no denying it: if not for the fact that it was already in the hands of a mainstream producer, it would have been something she would have loved to put her teeth into. For the sake of the script alone she agreed to meet up for coffee. To his credit, he hadn't wasted her time with silly chitchat, but instead had gotten right down to business. Before their coffee had been served he had offered her the job of directing the movie, emphasizing the fact that she would have a big budget at her disposal. The idea of being able to work without having to be restricted by a cripplingly low budget had been tempting, but not enough to convince her to ignore her trepidation. Then as a final attempt to reel her in, he had suggested that she at least come over to France, where most of the movie was going to be shot, for a few weeks to meet everybody and to get the feel of the project. He promised he would reimburse her for any expenses, no strings attached, and if she still wasn't interested, well, then that would be that. Against her better judgment she had agreed and now, after only being there one week, she'd had it. This just wasn't her style.

She was used to working with a small, dedicated crew who, despite the restrictions of a low budget, tried to tell the story the way they thought the story should be told, without bias. Of course everybody hoped that the movie would make money, just like these people did, but that never influenced the artistic choices they made. That was the way she liked it. It was the way she thought a movie should be made. On this project there were just too many investing parties meddling with the creative process. She reached for the telephone next to the bed. She'd made up her mind: she was going back home on the first available flight. Kees had said at their first meeting that he'd got other directors lined up. Well, one of them could do it, she thought, and get rich fast. She wished them luck.

❖

Lizzy threw her bags into the trunk of her car and planted herself behind the steering wheel relieved to be back on home soil. Her family had immigrated to the Netherlands when she was just four years old, and although she was proud of her British roots, Holland was the only home she'd known, and it was where she felt she belonged. She turned the key in the ignition, pressed Play on her CD player, and to the sound of Fleetwood Mac, she drove out of the airport parking lot.

She loved driving this time of night. There were fewer cars, and the backdrop of lights along the main roads always created in her mind the illusion that the road belonged to her, that it was lit up especially for her to follow. It gave her the feeling that she was free to go anywhere she liked. She thought back to when she and Maurice would get in the car late at night. They'd head for the highway and drive for ages, making up destinations as they went along. When they got tired they'd stop for coffee and then head back. She would give anything to be able to travel back through time to one of those moments. This time they'd drive on, never stopping, never turning back. They'd find a different destination.

Forty minutes later she was climbing the four flights of narrow stairs leading up to her apartment. It was the one thing that had made her think twice before buying the place. Maurice hadn't been put off by them and had insisted that they'd get used to them and that after a while they wouldn't even notice them. That had been nearly eight years ago, and Lizzy still noticed them. She unlocked her front door and stepped into the familiar dark hallway, automatically dropping her bags under the coat rack. As she turned to close the door she heard a sound from behind her. Her heart missed a beat as she abruptly turned around to face the darkened hallway.

"Who's there?"

She instinctively reached out and felt for the light switch, and the blinding void of darkness disappeared. At the end of the hall stood a woman with shoulder-length auburn hair, wearing a dressing gown identical to Lizzy's, holding a broom tightly to her chest and looking just as terrified as Lizzy felt.

"Who the hell are you?"

"I'm…I'm…are you Lizzy?"

Lizzy's brain raked through its memory banks, but she couldn't remember ever meeting this woman before. The stranger did not wait for her answer, but quickly continued.

"Chris never got through to you, did he? Oh God, this is so embarrassing. He said he'd make sure he got in contact with you."

It was clear by her expression and tone of voice that she was more than a little upset, and hearing her mention Chris's name only added to Lizzy's confusion. "Chris let you in?"

She nodded sheepishly and Lizzy studied her, unsure what to think. She thought she knew all of Chris's friends, but friend or no friend, it still didn't explain what she was doing in her home.

"How do you know Chris?"

"We met at his last exhibition, at the Pumpkin Gallery."

Lizzy suddenly remembered Chris telling her about another fellow Brit he'd met during his last exhibition. He'd been showing the work of a young unknown artist in his gallery and apparently she had been the only person to walk in off the street and fully grasp the meaning of his work. They had hit it off and met up frequently to talk about art. She remembered Chris telling her that she always seemed a little anxious, but that he always found her conversation refreshing as well as engaging. Lizzy consulted her memory again trying to remember what her name had been.

"Is your name Judith?"

The woman looked surprised. "Yes. Judith Hilford."

Although she was a stranger to her, just being able to place her as an acquaintance of Chris relieved some of the tension Lizzy felt. She had no idea what had possessed Chris to leave her in her home, but the mere fact that he had, proved to her that she could at least be trusted. She started to take off her jacket.

"This is so awful, I'm so sorry. You must be so angry."

Lizzy hung her jacket on one of the remaining hooks. "No, no, I'm not angry. Surprised, but not angry, and I wouldn't call it awful, just a new experience to add to the list."

Judith's expression was still one of utter shock and she was still gripping the broom tightly to her chest. Suddenly the idea that Judith would consider her a threat in her own home, holding nothing more than a broom to defend herself against her, seemed somehow kind of funny. Lizzy couldn't help but smile as she approached her.

"Well, Judith, I'm feeling slightly dehydrated and I'm dying for a decent cup of tea, so why don't you put down the broom and join me for a drink and you and I get better acquainted?"

Judith's face turned red as she lessened her grip on the broom.

Lizzy passed her and headed straight for the kitchen wondering why Chris would have let her into her home. One thing she knew for sure: there had better be a good reason or she'd kill him. She would have called him right then and there, but she knew he was already away on vacation and wouldn't be back for another three weeks.

Although she knew there shouldn't be any fresh milk in the refrigerator, she opened it anyway. After all, there shouldn't be anybody in her home, but there was. As expected, there wasn't any. In fact, the refrigerator was as bare as she'd left it. She wondered how many days this woman had been here and what she'd eaten. She closed the refrigerator door and opened a cupboard on the other side of the kitchen where she always kept a reserve bottle of coffee creamer for moments like these when she ran out of milk.

Judith entered the living room just as Lizzy was pouring the hot water into the mugs. Her hair was now tied back and she'd changed out of the dressing gown into a smart pair of light brown pants and a white blouse that hung loose. She looked elegant in a fumbled kind of way and Lizzy could tell by the way she walked toward her that she was still feeling uneasy.

"Do you take sugar and milk?"

"Neither, thank you."

Lizzy spooned out the teabags and passed a mug across the counter to Judith.

"So, how long have you been here?"

"Four days."

Lizzy added two spoons of sugar and poured coffee creamer

into her own mug and noticed Judith's expression. She knew that a lot of people found the idea of coffee creamer in tea disgusting and normally she felt compelled to explain how she hated black tea, but this time she felt it unnecessary and let the moment pass. She joined Judith in the living room and sat in her favorite spot next to the fireplace. Judith seated herself on the couch opposite.

"Do you mind if I smoke?"

Judith seemed surprised at the question. "No, of course not."

Lizzy took out a cigarette and lit it up. She hadn't had one since an hour before the plane had taken off, nearly four hours ago. She took a long drag and breathed contentedly.

"I'm sorry I used your dressing gown. I was in the bathroom when I heard the door. It was the first thing at hand."

"Don't worry about it. I never use it anyway. It was given to me by a friend as a birthday present, but I don't feel comfortable in it. I only kept it out of politeness for when she visits." Lizzy took another drag of her cigarette. "May I ask why it is you're here? Or is it too personal?"

"Well, it's personal, but I think you're owed an explanation."

"Not necessarily." Lizzy took another drag of her cigarette. "So Chris let you in?"

"Yes. He said you'd be away for a few weeks and that he would okay it with you. I am truly sorry about this."

Lizzy knew Chris wouldn't have been able to reach her.

"I'm sure he tried, but I'd forgotten to pack my cell phone."

"Oh, I see."

Lizzy studied her a moment. It was clear she was nervous and she wondered what Judith was really thinking.

"How long were you planning on staying?"

"Well, Chris said you'd be gone for three weeks, so I assumed we'd be here for another two."

Lizzy noticed the "we" bit and was surprised to think that there might be somebody else in the apartment.

"We?"

Judith quickly explained. "My daughter, Emily. She's only seven." She diverted her gaze. "She's sleeping at the moment."

It had already been a surprise to come home and find a stranger standing in her hallway, but the idea that a young child was asleep under her roof was somehow more unsettling. "Are you going through some kind of breakup?"

Judith simply nodded her reply without looking up. Lizzy settled farther back in her chair and let the idea sink in. She wasn't in the mood for company, especially that of people she didn't know, but Judith had thought she had two weeks, and she had a kid. Lizzy knew that Chris would not have brought her there if he hadn't thought it necessary. She suddenly felt very tired, too tired to have to deal with this woman's predicament.

Judith spoke up. "Look, I'm truly sorry about this. Really I am. If I had known you didn't know we were here, then I would never have come. If you would just allow us to stay the night, I assure you we'll leave first thing tomorrow morning."

Lizzy took another drag of her cigarette and figured what the hell. After all, she couldn't put a woman and child onto the street with nowhere to go.

"Well, I know Chris wouldn't have let you into my home without good reason, so you're welcome to stay the two weeks."

Judith shook her head adamantly. "No. You're being very kind, but I can't ask you to do this."

"Do you have anywhere else to stay?"

Judith averted her eyes again.

"And besides, you didn't ask. I offered."

"Yes, but it's not fair to you. You've come home and found two complete strangers sleeping in your home. I'm not sure I would have reacted as hospitably as you if it had happened to me."

Lizzy put out her cigarette.

"Well, no harm has been done, so I guess it would be egotistical of me not to be. Look, things are as they are. It will probably be awkward at times, especially because we don't know each other, but we can take it day by day. I'm not home that often anyway due to my work, so you'll have the place pretty much to yourselves. As long as we respect each other, I'm sure it will be okay."

Judith chewed the inside of her mouth. "I haven't enough money to—"

Lizzy interjected. "You don't need to pay me to stay here. Like I said, you're welcome to stay. Just focus on what you need to do for you and your daughter."

The sudden wave of anguish she saw on Judith's face made her feel very uncomfortable and she quickly stood. "Well, if you'll excuse me, I'm going to bed. I have a busy day ahead of me tomorrow. It was nice meeting you, Judith." Before Judith could say anything else, Lizzy left the room.

Judith remained seated, mulling over what had just happened. She felt so pathetic and embarrassed and wondered what Lizzy must think of her. She couldn't believe that she had meant what she'd said when she said they could stay for the two weeks. It was an incredibly kind offer. She felt angry at herself for being in this position. Why hadn't she stayed and asked Menno to leave? She hadn't even tried. She'd just packed her bags and run away without any plan, like a silly teenager. She couldn't believe what she'd done and now Lizzy, a complete stranger, was saddled up with a penniless woman and her daughter. Lizzy had said it would be egotistical of her not to be hospitable; well, it would be selfish of Judith to stay. She should go back and face Menno properly and ask him to leave, but even as she thought it she knew she couldn't.

She just couldn't trust herself. He'd either start on one of his raving monologues or convince her to get back with him, and she couldn't cope with either. Something had snapped inside her, dead, closed for good. There was no way she could go back home. There was no way of getting around it; she would have to swallow her pride and call her sister. She'd done this to herself, so it was her responsibility to deal with the consequences. Not Emily or Lizzy or anybody else. The clock on top of the fireplace told her it was twelve minutes past one. She picked up Lizzy's mug and swilled it out along with her own before turning off the lights, and as she headed down the hall toward her bedroom, she wondered how on earth anyone could drink coffee creamer in their tea.

CHAPTER THREE

Lizzy reluctantly woke to the annoying high-pitched buzzing of her alarm clock. She hated the penetrating sound and she hated even more that she had to have it on loud, otherwise she'd sleep right through it. Only half-conscious, she stretched out her arm and after a few seconds of fumbling misses managed to switch the wretched thing off. The silence that followed was a welcoming invitation to sleep again, but her sense of responsibility managed to make itself heard, reminding her that she had a lot of catching up to do. As she lay there, slowly resigning herself to the fact that she had to get up, she became, as usual, acutely aware of the empty space beside her. She didn't need to look to know it was empty. Every fiber of her being felt it. She had, at one time, considered buying a new bed, but that would have meant accepting that the memories really were just memories. She flipped back the covers not wanting to think about the past and remembered that she wasn't alone in the apartment.

She remembered her initial shock at finding a stranger in her home and remembered the scared look on Judith's face and the conversation that ensued. Judith had seemed nice enough and had clearly been more distressed about the situation than she had been. *Judith, Judith the art connoisseur.* Lizzy cringed. *Mother of a seven-year-old.* She gathered the breakup must have been pretty bad for her to take her daughter and camp out in a stranger's home. For a moment she thought about the different possible scenarios, but the visions this evoked were unwelcome ones and she did not yet feel ready to cope with the harsh realities of the world so early in the morning.

Being able to stand under her own clean shower instead of that of an unfamiliar French hotel room was a refreshing antidote against her lethargy, and by the time she was dressed she felt more prepared to face the day ahead. She started down the hall on her way to the kitchen for her usual morning cup of tea, and recognized the distinct sound of a cartoon as she approached the living room. A little girl dressed in pink pajamas was sitting on the couch engrossed in a cartoon. Lizzy remained in the doorway feeling awkward and uncertain what to do. The little girl looked her way and seemed to freeze. Lizzy quickly decided it would be best to act casual and approached her trying to sound disarming.

"Hello there. You must be Emily." She held out her hand. "I'm Lizzy, I live here."

The little girl gaped up at her with a look of fright and Lizzy wondered where Judith was as she tried to come up with something reassuring. "I'm a friend of your mother's."

Emily's face relaxed slightly and she cautiously shook Lizzy's hand. Lizzy recognized the cartoon blaring on the screen in front of them.

"Ah, *Scooby-Doo*, that's my favorite cartoon."

Emily's eyes widened and a smile lit up her face. Lizzy knew she'd broken the ice and felt she could now safely head for the kitchen. When she looked back into the living room she saw that Emily was now standing at the side of the couch watching her. She'd never felt comfortable around children and now was no different.

"Do you really like cartoons?" Emily asked cautiously.

"Some of them I do. *Scooby-Doo, Spider-Man…*"

"Spider-Man!" Emily giggled. "But that's for boys!"

Lizzy pretended to be insulted. "Who said so?"

"Everybody knows that!"

"They do, do they? Well, they don't know what they're talking about!"

Emily giggled, and it was clear from her expression that Lizzy's answers were unprecedented.

"So what's your favorite cartoon?"

"*Pokémon.*" Her response was quick as if she'd been waiting for the question and Lizzy pretended to think a moment before speaking again.

"Nah, *Scooby-Doo* is way better than *Pokémon.*"

"No, it isn't!" she excitedly exclaimed, obviously thrilled to be having such a conversation with a grown-up.

Lizzy was about to lay out her case and defend *Scooby-Doo*, when Judith entered the room. She looked tired and pale and Lizzy got the impression that she had dressed quickly. Judith glanced briefly in her direction as she approached Emily.

"Hey, you, you're supposed to be dressed by now." She gave Emily a kiss on top of her head. "Go on and get changed and I'll make you some breakfast, and don't forget to brush your teeth."

"Okay, Mommy." Emily ran out of the room and Judith turned to face Lizzy, self-consciously pushing back a strand of hair that seemed intent on hanging free.

"I'm sorry about that. I don't usually oversleep."

"There's nothing to be sorry about. I think you have a lovely daughter."

"Thank you. Do you mind if I make some toast?"

"No, of course not."

Judith joined her in the kitchen and started making some toast. It reminded Lizzy that the cupboards were virtually empty and that she needed to go to the store.

"I'm planning on getting some shopping in later. Is there anything in particular that I should get for you and Emily?"

"Oh no, thank you. You don't have to worry about us. I've decided to call my sister and ask if we can stay there."

Lizzy wondered why, if that was an option, she hadn't done it in the first place. "You're planning on going today?"

"Well, I was thinking of tomorrow, if that's okay with you?"

Lizzy shrugged. "Sure."

Just then Emily ran back into the room wearing a pretty pink floral dress. Lizzy wondered if she ever wore anything besides pink. She didn't usually like the color, but she did think Emily looked cute in it.

"Now, that was way too fast for you to have washed and brushed. Never mind. You can do it after your breakfast."

Lizzy sat at the dining table with her mug of tea sorting through the mountain of accumulated mail from the past week. As she did, she was very aware of Emily sitting at the kitchen counter munching on a piece of toast while telling her mother something that had happened at school. The two of them were in their own bubble, safe and content with one another. A perfect and natural image of a mother and her child together, and yet somehow it seemed utterly surreal to Lizzy. For a moment she imagined it was Maurice in the kitchen talking to a little girl, but she instantly felt the familiar jab of guilt in her chest. It was time to leave. She forced the image from her mind and tried to sound cheerful as she left the table.

"Well, I'm off. You're sure you don't need anything from the supermarket?"

Judith smiled politely. "No, we're fine, but thank you for offering."

"Okay, well, good luck with calling your sister." She turned to leave and as she did, gave Emily a little wave. Emily waved back with a big grin as she bit into another slice of toast.

❖

There was no other reason to delay making the phone call. She'd dropped Emily off at school, Lizzy was out, and she had to face the fact that there was nowhere else for them to stay. She took a few deep breaths in an attempt to calm her nerves and then dialed her sister's number. She waited anxiously as the ring tone repeated itself several times. She was about to hang up when a curt-sounding male answered. "Jacob van Baarn speaking."

"Hello, Jacob?" She paused. "It's Judith." She listened to the silence and quickly added, "Catherine's sister?"

"Oh! Judith!" Although he was momentarily taken aback, he remained just as curt and emotionless as before. "Catherine isn't here at the moment. She's gone skiing with some friends in Austria." He paused before continuing. "She won't be back until Friday. Would you like me to pass on a message?"

Judith's heart sank even further.

"No. No, thank you. I'll call her when she's back."

"As you wish. Good day."

Judith was about to say good-bye but didn't get the chance; he'd already hung up and she was left with the sound of his voice echoing in her head. She had never liked him. From the first moment she had laid eyes on him at one of her sister's teen parties she had been amazed at his arrogance and the amount of pretentiousness he oozed. She had instinctively disliked him and had known right then that her sister would marry him.

From somewhere far above her head a plane roared through the sky. She felt small and insignificant, a stranger to the world. It felt like she'd jumped off a sinking ship onto a shrinking island, and she was angry with herself; angry, because she was at a loss at what to do next. For a moment she considered calling Menno, but she knew there was no going back. She placed the phone back in its holder and told herself it was time for her to gain control. She knew she should have gone to the job center the very same day she had left him, but the whole task had been too daunting. She hadn't worked outside the house since before Emily was born and she had panicked, feeling totally inadequate, but she had neither the time nor the money to succumb to fear or self-doubt. *Judith, you have a child to consider and she is counting on you*, she told herself as she pulled on her coat and left the apartment.

❖

Lizzy had spent most of her morning letting members of her crew know she was back in town and available again. She'd been to the warehouse they had chosen as their primary shooting location to see how the building of the set was coming along, and after having spent a few hours there had tried to reach Anita, her producer, but hadn't been able to get a hold of her. She had been able to reach Sam, her storyboard artist, and had set up a meeting for later that afternoon to go over the latest sketches. Finding herself with a few hours to spare, she decided to go back home to do some work on the shooting script.

As she opened her front door she caught the lingering scent of an unfamiliar perfume. Although it was nothing like Maurice's, it reminded her of how much she still missed the familiar delicate trail of her scent that had once tinted every room. Feelings of want and loneliness engulfed her as she imagined Maurice welcoming her home again. The black hole inside her chest stirred and she struggled to block it out.

She nearly didn't notice the note Judith had left her on the kitchen counter.

Dear Lizzy,

I have not been able to contact my sister and I would like to take you up on your generous offer if it still stands. I truly am sorry to have put you in this situation.

Judith

Lizzy read the note a second time and wondered if she had done the right thing in offering to let them stay for another two weeks, but as she was in no mood for inner reflection, quickly decided that what was done was done and that it was best not to think about it. After Judith had said that she and Emily didn't need anything from the store, Lizzy had forgotten all about getting some shopping in. She rarely ate at home nowadays and only bought the bare necessities, often late at night on her way home, but she felt obligated to make sure there was food for her temporary cohabitants whether they wanted it or not.

She spent way more time in the supermarket than she'd anticipated. She had never gotten used to buying for one and now she was trying to think for three, and that was proving equally difficult. She had no idea what they liked and eventually decided on buying what she liked and then tripling it, including some junk food she thought Emily might like.

The apartment was still empty when she got back, so after unpacking the shopping she wrote a note to Judith letting her know there was food in the cupboards and to feel free to help themselves, then left to meet Sam.

❖

Judith felt completely done in. She hadn't expected it to be easy, but she hadn't been prepared for the humiliation. She'd trudged around to every employment agency listed in the area and had filled in the same monotonous forms, answered the same repetitive questions to a seemingly uninterested person behind a computer every time. Only after they had entered her details into their computer did they tell her that they didn't have anything to offer her at the moment. Apparently there were more applicants than there were job offers in the field she was looking for. They also kindly pointed out that it was especially difficult in her case, because she had been out of the sector for so long. She had kept up a brave face and had made it clear to all of them that she was prepared to do any type of work if need be.

After this humiliating morning of job hunting with nothing to show for it, she'd made her way down to social services to talk about the possibility of benefits. She had been made to wait forever before actually getting to speak to someone, and when she did it had been a very young woman who had asked personal questions with a mixed attitude of complacency and judgmental suspicion.

The young woman had not been able to give her any guarantees and Judith had left there with a pile of forms to fill in and an even greater feeling of helplessness. She hadn't been naïve in thinking she'd find a job immediately and hadn't expected to walk out of the building with cash in hand, but the whole experience had made her feel completely inadequate and a long way away from being anywhere.

She noticed that Lizzy's coat wasn't hanging on the coat rack and felt relieved to have some time to herself to think and find some composure again without having to find the energy for awkward socializing. When she saw the paper on top of the kitchen counter she figured that Lizzy hadn't been back yet, but then she noticed something had been written under the message she had left.

> *I'm sorry you weren't able to contact your sister, and yes, my offer still stands. There's food in the cupboards. Feel free to help yourself.*
> *Lizzy*

Lizzy's note instantly brought tears to her eyes. After the indifference of the people she'd spoken to throughout the day, Lizzy's selfless gesture and the relief it brought overwhelmed her. She sat and stared at the words Lizzy had written. She had done nothing but impose herself upon Lizzy and yet she'd been nothing but kind about it. Lizzy's kindness somehow made her feel even more guilty and pathetic than she already did. She fought hard not to cry, not wanting to feel sorry for herself, and after a few moments of internal battle, wiped away her tears and rose to her feet again. She opened the refrigerator door and was greeted by the wonderful sight of shelves stuffed with a variety of healthy products, which filled her with a pulse of confidence. Menno had always controlled the finances, and when she'd left him she'd done so with very little money. She had stretched it the best she could over the past few days, but not knowing how she was going to feed Emily once it ran out had torn at her heart.

The prospect of being able to prepare Emily a fresh and nutritious meal made her feel more like a normal mother again. After further inspection she decided she would cook schnitzels for dinner. She hesitated when taking them out of the freezer, unsure whether she should cook for Lizzy as well or if Lizzy even expected it. She decided it was the politest thing to do considering what she had done for them and figured that Lizzy could warm it up later if she wanted it or simply put it back in the freezer as a reserve meal if she didn't.

❖

Lizzy finally left Sam's around nine. They'd been working on the storyboard all afternoon and although there was still work to be done, they had decided to call it quits for the night and to carry on tomorrow. On the way home she stopped to pick up a burger and some fries. She didn't particularly want it, but she knew she needed to eat something and if she waited until she got home she wouldn't be in the mood for making anything.

The apartment was quiet and most of the lights were off, so she guessed that Judith and Emily had gone to bed already. She dropped her take-away on the kitchen counter and noticed that Judith had written her another note.

Dear Lizzy,

Thank you for your hospitality. I made Emily and myself schnitzels. I didn't know whether you would want one or not so I made you one just in case. It's in the microwave.

I have no words to describe how grateful I am. I can only promise you that I will repay you as soon as possible.

Judith

Lizzy felt pleased with herself. She had obviously done the right thing in buying the groceries. She opened the microwave door and took out the plate: schnitzel, mashed potatoes, and green beans. She hadn't had a proper home-cooked meal in ages, and with a little anticipation placed the plate back in the microwave and warmed it up.

It felt weird eating a meal cooked by a stranger in her own home, but there was no denying it, the meal was delicious. She remembered a book she'd once read, *Peace Is Every Step* by a Buddhist named Thich Nhat Hanh. It was a book about how to implement ways of achieving inner peace. In it he mentioned eating mindfully. A person could get the fullest nourishment from food by taking the time to imagine where it came from while eating it. She was unsuccessfully trying to imagine a potato still in the earth when she realized she was not alone.

"Is it all right?" Judith nodded toward Lizzy's plate.

Lizzy quickly tried to swallow the mouthful she had just popped into her mouth.

"Yes, very nice, thank you."

"I didn't know whether you would want it, but I thought I'd take the risk."

"I'm glad you did. I hadn't expected it, but it was a nice surprise. The dinner I'd expected is over there." Lizzy nodded in the direction of the take-away bag still standing on the counter.

"So I take it you're not planning on eating it?"

"God no, this is enough for me."

"Would you mind if I had it? I feel a bit peckish."

"No, please help yourself. It will only go to waste otherwise."

Judith walked over to the kitchen counter and unpacked the bag.

"How was your day?"

"Oh please, I don't want to bore you."

"You won't. I'm interested."

Judith joined her at the table. "Well, to be honest, not as good as I'd hoped for."

"How come?" Lizzy took another bite of her schnitzel, this time a more polite portion.

"I tried to get in contact with my sister this morning, but apparently she's away on some skiing trip. Then I went out hunting for a job, unsuccessfully I might add, and then I went to social services and came back with a lot of uncertainties and a pile of forms to fill in."

"I take it the job agency didn't have anything for you?"

"Nothing in the field I was hoping for, anyway."

"What field is that?"

"Teaching."

"And you'd like to teach again?"

"I think so. It was what I studied for, but it's been such a long time since I last stood in front of a class."

"Why'd you give it up?"

"To be able to spend more time with my daughter. What about you, Chris said you were a movie director?"

Lizzy noticed the swift diversion, but respected it. "I'm what they call an independent moviemaker."

"Sounds exciting. What does that mean exactly?"

"It means I get to do whatever I want as a director as long as it doesn't exceed the budget that I and a few others have managed to scrape together."

"Sounds challenging."

Lizzy realized she was seeing Judith smile properly for the first time.

"It is."

"How many movies have you made?"

"Two. We're just about to start shooting on the third."

"What's it about?"

"It's about the life of Alice James, the youngest sister of Henry James."

"I've never heard of her."

"Most people haven't. That's why we want to tell her story."

"What's so special about her?"

"She was the youngest sister of the novelist Henry James and is considered by some to be a feminist of the nineteenth century. She was a teacher like you, but she never married and chose the company of one particular woman. She was often plagued with illness and suffered from nervous breakdowns, but she kept a diary in which she portrayed her views on social conformity. Her depictions of invalidism and the role of women within the family and society give us a deeper insight into the lives of women in that time."

"I'm intrigued."

"You're supposed to be."

"Mommy!"

Judith jumped to her feet and Lizzy followed her as she rushed down the hall to Emily's bedroom. Emily was sitting bolt upright in bed, breathing fast, soaked with sweat and clearly terrified. Lizzy watched from the doorway as Judith quickly wrapped her up in her arms, rocking her and whispering soft, soothing words. Lizzy felt superfluous and whispered, "Is there anything I can do?"

Judith shook her head in reply and gently kept rocking Emily in her arms. Realizing there was nothing she could do, Lizzy left them alone and stepped out onto the balcony. She lit a cigarette, wondering what could cause such a little girl to have nightmares.

Before going to bed she popped her head around the corner of Emily's room and found Judith asleep on the bed with Emily still in her arms. It was an endearing image, one that captivated her. Maurice had wanted a child. Maurice had wanted to be in this picture. Why had she let her own fear deny Maurice her dream? She felt the black hole in her chest start to churn again. She grabbed an extra blanket from the cupboard and placed it over Judith. She decided to leave the hall light on. If Emily awoke again, she thought it best that it shouldn't be in the dark.

CHAPTER FOUR

The next five days left Lizzy little time to think about her guests. Word of her return had spread fast and her time was no longer her own. Everybody needed her opinion or her approval on something, from choosing the position of a chair on set to helping out with wardrobe. Each day she'd left the apartment at six and hadn't gotten back until midnight, and at the end of each long day she had arrived home late to find her guests asleep and a dinner waiting for her in the microwave.

At first she'd felt awkward about it, not wanting Judith to feel obligated to cook for her, but as soon as she got in her car and headed for home, she would wonder what dinner lay waiting for her. She hadn't seen either Judith or Emily throughout this time, and she wondered how Judith was doing in her search for a job and a place to live. Twice she had awoken to the sound of Emily calling for her mother in the middle of the night and both times she had stayed in bed and listened as Judith quietly but quickly crossed the hall to Emily's room. Both times she had fallen asleep feeling sorry for her.

Thinking everybody was asleep, Lizzy quietly entered the apartment, but to her surprise found Judith sitting on the couch reading a book and unintentionally made her jump.

"Sorry. I didn't mean to startle you."

"No, I'm sorry. I didn't hear you come in. I must have lost track of time."

Lizzy recognized the book. *The Moonstone* by Wilkie Collins. "No wonder you lost track of time. It's a great book, a real page turner."

"Yes. I mean, I've only just started, but his style is so captivating. I don't normally read mystery novels, but I was scanning your bookshelves and this seemed well read and I fancied something different. I hope you don't mind."

"No, not at all. Books are meant to be read, especially books like that. Tea?"

Judith smiled. "You drink a lot of tea, don't you?"

"Yes, I do. When I'm not drinking coffee, that is," Lizzy added as she started for the kitchen.

"Well, you've had a long day. I'm sure you'd like some time to yourself."

"No, it's fine. You don't have to disappear just because I'm back." Lizzy was surprised at her own words and even more surprised to realize she'd meant it. "And besides, I wanted to thank you for the lovely meals."

"There's spaghetti Bolognese in the microwave."

Lizzy opened the microwave door and peeped in at her meal. She couldn't remember when she'd last eaten spaghetti Bolognese, and yet it had always been one of her favorite dishes. She closed the microwave door and pressed the three-minute button.

"I'm really grateful for this and I think your cooking is great, but I don't want you feeling obligated to cook for me."

Judith twisted around to face her, resting her arms on the back of the sofa.

"I like to cook and, if you don't mind my saying, your eating habits could do with some improving."

"We hardly know each other and yet you're already noticing my bad habits!" Lizzy teased.

Judith blushed slightly. "I'm sorry, that was rude. I didn't mean anything by it, I—"

Lizzy raised her hand. "I know you didn't. I was just teasing.

I'll be the first to admit that my eating pattern has always been a weak point of mine."

"How come?"

"I don't know. I just get distracted. No, that's a lie. I'm aware I should eat at certain moments, but I can't be bothered. I'd rather finish whatever it is I'm doing at that moment."

"Don't you get tired, though?"

"No. It's not as if I don't eat. I just seem to only eat when I can no longer ignore my hunger, and then it's mostly take-away."

"I couldn't live like that. I enjoy food too much and enjoy preparing it. As a child I was fascinated with cooking. I used to go down to the kitchen and watch as dinner was being prepared. I don't know why, but I was always fascinated by the big pots and pans, the smells and the idea of chopping things. At the age of eight I decided I was going to have the biggest kitchen in the world."

Lizzy laughed. "And did you get it?"

"No, thank God. I soon realized the bigger the kitchen, the bigger the cleanup was most likely to be."

Lizzy's meal was done and she settled down on one of the remaining couches.

"So how's the job hunting been going?"

Judith shook her head. "Not so good. There's apparently little demand for an art teacher at the moment, but I've told them I'll take any job that comes along."

Two things rushed through Lizzy's mind simultaneously. First, the delicious taste of the Bolognese in her mouth, and second, the pity she felt for Judith, knowing all too well what it felt like not being able to do what one felt passionate about.

"So how did you come to be an art teacher?"

Judith took a sip of her tea before answering. "Mrs. Eijk."

Lizzy made a questioning face as she munched on a mouthful of gorgeous Bolognese.

"She was my art teacher in high school. She was wonderfully eccentric and kind. Her character was completely out of place at the private school I attended. I was mesmerized by her: the way she dressed, the way she spoke, her passion for art. She instilled in me an undeviating love for it and I wanted to be just like her. I did my best to please her and studied the subject vigorously outside of classes. I suppose you could say I even had a little schoolgirl's crush on her, but it was more than that. I was very disciplined at school and did well in all of my classes, but I had fallen in love with art and painting. Mrs. Eijk said I had a natural talent for it, but that it was a craft you had to practice, and so I did. I got better and better at it and found that a certain peace and serenity took hold of me when I painted. Of course, as I grew older my own character evolved and I realized I couldn't be as eccentric as her, because it wasn't in my character to be so. I also found out that it isn't easy to earn a living as an artist, so I decided to become a teacher and teach others the beauty of art and help them find their artistic talents. So that's how I became an art teacher."

Lizzy was touched by the innocence of Judith's story and by the openness with which she had told it.

"Didn't you miss it, then?"

"Well yes, but I've never regretted stopping. Being a good mother to Emily is the most important thing in the world to me. I wanted to spend as much time as possible with her while she was growing up, I still do, and I was fortunate enough to have that luxury up until now. And you? What made you want to be an independent moviemaker?"

"That's hard to explain. I've always been fascinated with storytelling. Originally in book form, which later progressed into moviemaking. I became fascinated by the concept of taking a story and making it come to life through real-life moving imagery. That and the fact I believe it's a great way of teaching people things they otherwise wouldn't know or think about. I mean, there are so many reasons why a person doesn't learn more about a subject: they're either too tired or can't be bothered, ignorant, or simply incapable in some way. Movies can reach these people sitting in their chairs at home and show them things they would otherwise never have known about. Movies can help create understanding and insight, even help change minds about fundamental stuff and, of course, let's not forget, movies can be just damn good fun."

"That's true, although I have to admit, it's been a long time since I actually sat down to watch one."

Lizzy placed her empty plate down on the coffee table.

"Can I ask you a question?"

"Sure."

"How come Emily has nightmares?"

Judith took a long breath before answering. "Well, according to the doctor, she has suppressed anxiety."

"Anxiety for what?"

Judith's expression turned sullen, making Lizzy wish she hadn't asked the question.

"It's all right you know. You don't have to answer me. I didn't mean to pry."

"No, I know you didn't. It's just easier not to think of things than face the truth of the matter sometimes, but it's time I started accepting the truth and deal with it."

Lizzy didn't quite know what to say. She agreed with what Judith said, but it stirred something deep inside her, something she didn't want stirred.

"The truth is, the relationship between Emily and her father... Who am I kidding, there is no relationship between them."

Judith's tears immediately made Lizzy feel claustrophobic.

"You don't have to tell me if you don't want to."

Judith quickly wiped the tears away. "I'm sorry. I don't normally cry so easily. I seem to be doing a lot of things lately I wouldn't normally do."

Lizzy wasn't sure what to say, but something Maurice used to say popped into her head and although she didn't want to, she felt compelled to say it to Judith.

"Someone used to tell me that everything happens for a reason.

We don't always know the reason at the time, but the ultimate intention is that we learn and move on into the next stage of our life, wiser than we were before."

"Do you believe that's true?"

Again Lizzy found herself at a loss for words. For years Maurice's proverb had made sense to her, but then Maurice had died and nothing had made sense anymore. It still didn't, but Lizzy didn't want to have to think about it. Not thinking about it was the only way she could keep her promise. The black hole inside her started to churn again and she could feel Judith studying her. Trying to ignore the discomfort, she managed to shrug in response to Judith's question.

Judith averted her gaze and started tracing an invisible line on the cover of the book that lay in her lap. "What if you don't want to enter the next stage? What if you feel you can't do it?"

Lizzy found Judith's gentle demeanor and humble honesty endearing, but the intimacy of the conversation was making the black hole in her chest churn even harder. She gave her the only answer she knew. "Just take it day by day." As soon as she said it, she knew she needed to leave the room before the dark abyss of emotion inside her pulled her in. She got up to leave, but before she left she felt compelled to say one more thing and forced herself to look at Judith.

"Whatever it is you're doing, Judith, you seem to be doing it because you feel you must. You can't ask more than that of yourself."

With that said she quickly turned and headed for the sanctuary of her bedroom in the hope of finding her numbness again.

CHAPTER FIVE

Leaving Menno had been a big step, but Judith felt that she was no further than she had been the day she left him. Finding work and a place to live was proving more difficult than she had anticipated. The job agencies still didn't have any work for her, her application for welfare was still being processed, and her hunt for a place to live had been futile. She'd signed up for government housing, but the list was apparently so long it could take at least a year before she was eligible, and her attempt to find private housing had proved equally futile. There were places enough, but they were expensive and the landlords would only rent to people with paid jobs. She had three days left before her two-week arrangement with Lizzy ended. Time was running out.

She had hoped that she wouldn't have to call her sister again, but after another day of futile attempts at finding a place to live, she knew there was no way around it. She was jobless, penniless, and soon to be homeless. She needed to get things sorted, quickly, for Emily's sake; there was no room for pride in the current equation. Mustering up the nerve yet again, she picked up the receiver and punched in her sister's number.

"The van Baarn residence, how may I help you?"

Judith felt a small relief that a housemaid had answered and not her brother-in-law again.

"I would like to speak to Catherine, please."

"Whom may I say is calling?"

Judith took a deep breath. "Her sister, Judith."

"One moment please."

There was a click and Judith listened to the silence that followed; then, after what seemed an eternity, she heard her sister's voice for the first time in ten years.

"Catherine van Baarn speaking."

Judith took one last long breath before speaking.

"Catherine, it's me, Judith."

There was a momentary silence before her sister's sharpness filled the void. "What do you want, Judith?"

There was no easy answer to the question, no masking of the truth. "I've broken up with Menno."

"So, you've finally come to your senses, have you?"

Her sister made no attempt to hide her gloating satisfaction, making Judith want to reach through the phone and strangle her, but she checked herself and concentrated on keeping calm. "I suppose you could put it that way."

"Hmm. I know you didn't just call me to tell me this bit of delightful news, so what is it you want?"

Judith took another deep breath. "Well, I—"

"Oh, let me guess, you need money, but you're forgetting something, dear. You walked out on your money, remember? Thought you were better than us, didn't you?"

"No, Catherine, it wasn't like that."

"Oh, that's exactly how it was, and now your plan has backfired and you think you can come crawling back."

Judith could feel her self-composure slipping away.

"For Christ's sake, Catherine, I have a child to think of."

"Oh yes, the child. Well, you should have followed my advice and gotten rid of it when you could have."

Judith could no longer contain her anger.

"She's not an *it*, her name is Emily, and she's the best thing that ever happened to me. You're her aunt, for God's sake. No, you know what? Forget it, I should have known better. Just forget I even called." Judith hung up and steadied herself against the table, trying to calm herself. Her body was shaking and she didn't know whether she wanted to cry or hit something.

"Are you okay?"

Judith spun around to find Lizzy standing in the doorway looking concerned. Judith quickly turned away from her, feeling exposed.

"Yes, I'm fine."

"You don't look it."

"Well I am, okay? I just need some time to myself." Judith forced her trembling legs to move and just about made it to her room before bursting into tears.

❖

Lizzy waited for the kettle to boil, mulling over the conversation she had just overheard. She gathered Judith must have been talking to her sister, because she'd used the word *aunt*. She didn't know anything about Judith's background or her family, but her sister didn't seem to be a nice woman and obviously had no feelings for Emily. Lizzy wondered whether she should go to Judith or to just leave her be. Judith had made it clear that she wanted to be alone, but something in Lizzy told her that it would be best if Judith talked about it. On the other hand, it wasn't any of her business and she wasn't sure if she could cope with Judith's sad emotions. She made an extra cup of tea and reluctantly headed for Judith's bedroom. Her knock on the door got no reply and was the excuse she needed to walk away, but something inside her stopped her from doing so and before she knew what she was doing, she carefully opened Judith's door.

Judith was seated on the edge of her bed with her head resting in her hands. Lizzy placed a mug of tea on the bedside table before sitting down on the floor against the opposite wall. Judith kept her head buried in her hands and for a few moments Lizzy simply watched her cry, unsure what to say.

"Do you want to talk about it?"

Judith slowly shook her head. "You don't want to hear it."

"I wouldn't have asked if I didn't," Lizzy replied gently.

Judith lifted her head. Her face was tear stricken.

"I thought…I just hoped that maybe, maybe she'd changed, you know?" Judith shook her head. "I'm an idiot. There's no denying it, I'm a total idiot." She buried her head in her hands again.

Lizzy had no idea what had happened to Judith or what she might have done to end up where she was now, but she felt sure that Judith wasn't an idiot.

"I may not know you well, Judith, but one thing I'm sure you're not, is an idiot. From what I've seen so far, you're an intelligent, loving, responsible mother, whose life seems to have changed one hundred and eighty degrees, but who is trying her best to make things right for herself and her daughter, and from what I could gather from that phone call, it's your sister who's an idiot, not you. Is there no one else you can turn to?"

Judith shook her head again.

"Your parents?"

"They have both passed away, but my mother wouldn't have helped anyway. She considered Menno beneath our family status. Can you believe that?" She shook her head. "And when I made it clear I wouldn't break up with him, she threw me out of the house and made it very clear I was never to come back again."

"And your father supported this?"

"He had already passed away by the time I met Menno. He was nothing like my mother and sister, though. He was a kind and gentle man. We were always close and I could talk to him about anything. I'm convinced he would have supported me, been happy for me. I mean, at the time I was happy. When I met Menno I really believed I'd met somebody with whom I could share the rest of my life. You know, explore the world together, start a family, and eventually end up as two oldies who still hold hands while walking down the street, like you still sometimes see."

Lizzy snorted. "The ideal family life: a rare oddity if ever there was one."

"Yes, but that was what I wanted and thought I'd found."

"So I take it your mother never met Emily?"

"No. I called the house and left a message as soon as I realized I was pregnant, but I never heard from her." Judith wiped her nose on a piece of tissue. "I'm not saying my mother was bad. She was good to me while I was growing up, but we never really connected. As a child I was aware that my mother's love was different from my father's, but it wasn't until I grew older that I came to realize what that difference was. My father loved me for who I was. My mother loved the idea of me. She had it all planned, you see, what my sister and I would be like and how we would live our lives. As long as I lived the life she thought I should, we were fine. She regarded it as a personal betrayal when I wouldn't give Menno up, and she never forgave me for it."

Lizzy shook her head in disgust. "And I take it your sister sided with your mother?"

"My sister, hah!" Judith laughed cynically. "Well, when she found out I was pregnant she was considerate enough to send me a short letter advising me to have an abortion."

Lizzy was dumbstruck. She couldn't believe the audacity of it, let alone the twisted thinking behind it. "That must have hurt!"

"At the time it did. I felt misunderstood and unjustly treated, but when I held Emily in my arms for the first time and thought of them, the pain was replaced with sorrow. That they rejected me was one thing, but that they rejected Emily, so innocent and pure, it just shut the book for me. I was no longer welcome in their world, and they were no longer welcome in mine."

Lizzy had always had trouble trying to understand how people could be so cold and cruel to one another. It was bad enough that Judith's family rejected her, but to deny Emily's right to exist— Lizzy just couldn't believe it.

"What have you told Emily?"

"That was the hardest thing. For years I dreaded the moment when I would have to explain to her the absence of a family. Even Menno didn't have contact with his family. Then one evening, when she was six, as I was tucking her into bed she told me how her friends talked about their grandparents and she asked me how come she didn't have any. So I tried to explain it in a way that she could understand without upsetting her. I told her, her grandfather, who was a good man, had gone to heaven before she was born and that she did have a grandma, but that her grandma wanted to keep me locked up in this big castle and that her father had rescued me."

Lizzy raised her eyebrows. "And she believed it?"

"Well, she accepted the story. She said if Grandma didn't like me, then she didn't like Grandma."

They both fell silent and Lizzy felt the urge to tell Judith she could stay longer, but she was worried about the implications for herself. If she offered, it would mean them staying most likely for quite a while, and having people stay in her home for a longer period of time was quite different from having them stay for only a few weeks, but the more she thought about it, the more it seemed the right thing to do.

"You know, you can stay here longer if you like, until you've got things properly sorted."

Judith looked at her with disbelief. "Do you know what you're offering?"

"Yes."

"Why? Why would you do this?"

"Why wouldn't I?"

Judith's expression turned pensive. "It could be a while. I have no idea how things are going to turn out."

"I know."

"Are you sure, I mean really sure?"

"The way I see it is that we've gotten along so far, and you need a place to build from and this is as good a place as any, considering."

"And what happens if our presence starts to annoy you?"

"That won't happen. I think as long as we're considerate with one another, like we have been, we'll be fine."

"I don't have any money to—"

"Don't worry about it. I'll make sure there's always food in the cupboards, and if you want I can lend you some money until you get sorted. It's not the greatest way, I know, but it's a start. What do you say?"

Judith grimaced. "I haven't always been so helpless, you know."

"I don't see you as helpless, Judith. I just see a woman who is trying to figure out in which direction her life is heading. There's no shame in that and there's no shame in accepting somebody's help."

The phone started to ring and Lizzy pulled herself to her feet. She knew it was Anita, her producer, because they'd arranged the call earlier in the day.

"It's up to you, Judith, but I meant what I said."

"I'll pay you back, I promise, every penny."

Lizzy understood that it was important to Judith that she believed her. "I'm sure you will."

"You're too kind, Lizzy."

Lizzy turned in the doorway. "There's no such thing, and besides, my offer is purely egoistical. I like your cooking." She caught a glimpse of Judith's smile before she raced off to take Anita's call, and despite her initial concern about letting them stay, felt good about being able to offer Judith the breathing space she needed.

CHAPTER SIX

For the first time since leaving Menno, Judith had managed a proper night's sleep. After her talk with Lizzy the previous night she had stayed in her room feeling too tired to do anything but sleep. She had decided to take Lizzy up on her generous offer—not that she felt she had much choice, but knowing that she and Emily had a place to stay until they could get their own place took a load off her shoulders. She now had the time at least to rethink her situation and come up with a new approach to solving her problems. That morning she had awoken early with an unexpected sense of newfound confidence. She had hoped to speak to Lizzy at breakfast, but Lizzy had still been asleep and by the time she returned from dropping Emily off at school, Lizzy had left for work. She decided to take advantage of her solitude and spoil herself with a long, hot shower.

As the hot rays of water cascaded down her body, her thoughts wandered to Lizzy. She was astounded that a person could be so generous to someone she didn't know. She thought back to the conversations they had had since their arrival. There was something about her demeanor that evoked trust, but there was also a barrier, a sort of invisible line that Lizzy drew around herself, separating her from the space around her. Then there were those moments when something in her demeanor would change. The gentle look in her eyes would harden and she would find a way to cut the conversation short and leave the room. Her generosity and her aloofness were a contradiction Judith couldn't quite understand. She was still thinking about her when she stepped out of the shower and realized that the phone was ringing. She grabbed a towel, flung it around her waist, and ran, dripping wet, to the living room, managing to reach the phone before it stopped ringing. She quickly picked up the receiver and remembered that this was Lizzy's home phone. She hesitated, not sure how she should address herself. Then, squirming at the inelegance of her choice, simply said: "Hello?"

"Miss Hilford?"

"Yes, speaking."

"It's Yvonne from Top Line Job Center. We may have something for you. An employee from one of the companies we represent, Care All Round, has fallen sick and they need an immediate replacement for this week. We know it's not in your field, but on your application form you indicated you were prepared to do other work."

"What would I be doing?"

"You'd basically be going into old people's homes and helping out with the general chores that they can't manage on their own. It's mostly cleaning."

Judith needed a moment to let it sink in. She'd never done this type of thing before and it was a far cry from teaching.

Yvonne continued. "They want you to start tomorrow at half past eight, and it's six hours a day, minimum pay."

Judith quickly did the math and decided she should be able to get Emily to school and make it on time. "Okay. I'll do it. Where do I have to go?"

Judith jotted down the details and thanked Yvonne before hanging up. It wasn't a teaching job, but she felt immensely grateful for the opportunity to earn some money.

❖

It was nearly midnight when Lizzy got back, so she was surprised when Judith greeted her in the hallway.

"Hi, you're up late."

"I couldn't sleep, and well, I was kind of waiting for you."

Lizzy was a little surprised by the statement, but guessed by the glint in her eye that she had some good news.

"What is it?"

"One of the job centers called me. I've got work."

"That's great, Judith." Lizzy felt relieved for her, understanding how important this news was.

Judith quickly continued. "It's only cleaning. I'm supposed to go into old people's homes and help them out, but it's a start, right?"

For a moment Lizzy hesitated, realizing Judith was relying on her for confirmation. A job meant money, a way to move on, but Lizzy knew that having to clean other people's homes could sometimes make a person feel small and insignificant—and even if the work itself didn't have that effect, people's attitudes often did. Lizzy's own mother had done the same type of work for a while after her own divorce. There had been times when she had had to swallow her pride and then there had been times when she had found the work rewarding. It had helped pay the bills, and she had done it for as long as it had been necessary.

Judith's expression changed and Lizzy realized she was taking too long to reply. She pushed her doubt aside and spoke enthusiastically.

"Absolutely, Judith! It's great news."

Judith seemed to relax again and at that moment Lizzy realized that Judith's emotions were very easily reflected in her face. A trait she found endearing.

They sat at the dinner table and while Judith told her in further detail what the lady from the job agency had said, Lizzy ate the shepherd's pie that Judith had made her.

"She also said that if I do well I might be able to get more hours. I mean, I know it's a far cry from teaching, but it's a job, and I'm going to need a job if I'm to find a place for Emily and myself, aren't I?"

Lizzy found it a shame that although Judith was excited about the job, she clearly feared putting too much emphasis on it.

"Going into people's homes to clean is very different from teaching, and it won't always be easy, but I think you have the right to be excited and that you should be and that you should see this as a stepping stone to better pastures."

Judith's face lit up. "Oh, Lizzy, that is such a lovely way of putting it."

Lizzy enjoyed witnessing Judith's delight and placed her knife and fork down feeling, for a brief moment, content.

"Jeez, Judith, you sure can cook."

"Your compliment is touching, but it's only a shepherd's pie, and an ordinary one at that."

It suddenly dawned on Lizzy that Judith had not believed her when she had complimented her on her cooking on previous occasions.

"I mean it, Judith."

Judith turned away, shyly. "I've been told often enough that my cooking is plain to know it is."

Lizzy looked at her empty plate trying to figure out how anybody could call what she had just eaten plain. She knew instinctively that it was Judith's ex who had convinced her of this, and she felt like giving him her fist to chew on.

"I'm sorry, Judith, but whoever told you that is a complete ass."

Judith burst out laughing. "Oh, I'm so sorry, but if you knew Menno then you'd understand why that's so funny."

Lizzy had already decided that she didn't like this Menno guy, and now finding out that he had deliberately tried to convince Judith that she couldn't cook only added to the feeling of animosity. He obviously didn't appreciate her and Lizzy wondered what it was about him that had attracted Judith in the first place. She hoped Judith knew she deserved better.

"Are you filing for divorce?"

She shook her head. "No, we never married. It's quite funny if you think about it. I eloped and left everything I knew to be able to marry him, and we never did get around to tying the knot."

Lizzy didn't think it was funny, but thought it rather sad.

"Have you spoken to him since you left?"

Judith shook her head. "No, I know I have to eventually, but I've been scared that he'll somehow convince me to go back. I did leave him a note, though, the day I left." She grimaced. "I feel a bit guilty about that. Ten years reduced to a simple good-bye note."

"Would you go back if he asked you?"

Judith drew an invisible pattern with her right hand on the table's surface. "I hope not."

"You hope not?" Lizzy was astounded by Judith's vulnerability.

"I don't trust my own resolve around him. He has this way of making me agree with him somehow."

"Well, you found the resolve to leave him."

"Yes, I did. The thing is I didn't leave him for me, I left him for my daughter."

"Some people would argue that's the same thing, coming from a mother."

Judith smiled faintly at Lizzy's remark.

"I did try to make it work. I kept thinking every couple has their problems, if I just try harder…" Judith shook her head. "I thought I was doing right by Emily by trying to make it work, but I didn't realize just how miserable her life had become until she started having nightmares and the doctor explained to me that she was suffering from anxiety." Judith paused and drew in a long breath before continuing. "Menno rarely acknowledges her presence, and when he does it's to scold her for something. According to the doctor, that and his overpowering nature when he's home is what makes Emily feel anxious. Although she's only seven she is aware that her father doesn't like her and a part of her thinks it's her fault. She wants to make it better, but doesn't know how to. According to the doctor, these feelings come to the surface when she's asleep. Hence the nightmares."

Lizzy, like most people she knew, didn't have good relations with her father, but thinking back to the few times she had interacted with Emily, she couldn't for the life of her imagine how anybody could dislike her, let alone her own father.

"How on earth can he not like her?"

"Because he's convinced I'm unfaithful to him and he doesn't believe she's his."

Judith didn't strike Lizzy as the cheating kind. "I take it his beliefs are misplaced?"

"I loved him. It never crossed my mind to have an affair. When we first started dating he would say that seeing how other men looked at me made him feel proud to have me standing at his side. I used to be flattered, but then as time went by his perception of how other men looked at me grew irrational. We'd go somewhere and he'd be all charming and nice, but as soon as we got back home he would accuse me of flirting. The more I denied his accusations, the more convinced he was and the angrier he became. I couldn't win. Nothing I said or did made any difference. Menno was the one who initially suggested that we try for a child, and I naïvely thought that maybe having a child together would change things, but when Emily was born his silly paranoia transferred onto her. He became fixated with the idea that she was the product of me being with another man."

Lizzy wasn't sure whether she should pity the man or to simply dislike him even more. "Jeez, Judith, he sounds like a really nice guy."

Judith looked remorseful. "There was a time when he was, or at least seemed to be."

"But you stayed with him for another seven years?"

"Well, he was the father of my child and I thought with enough love and patience we'd get through it, but like I said, when I realized that Emily was suffering I knew it was time to leave. I feel bad about leaving the way I did, but I knew I wouldn't keep up the nerve if I had to confront him." Judith shook her head. "It's strange talking to you about him. It's like I have this whole life that I remember, but that I don't feel happened. It must sound mad to you."

Lizzy knew exactly what she meant, but she didn't want to start thinking about that.

"Well, if it's any consolation, I think you're being very brave and you did the right thing in leaving him."

"Has anyone ever told you you're a good listener?"

Lizzy felt a wave of sadness wash over her. Maurice used to tell her all the time. For a moment Lizzy held Judith's gaze, noticing for the first time that she had chestnut-colored eyes. Their warmth invited her to share her past and for a fleeting moment Lizzy considered telling Judith about Maurice, but then fear took hold of her as she realized that meant revealing how she felt, and the idea of baring her true feelings to anyone, let alone someone she barely knew, was overwhelming. She looked at her watch, pretending to notice the time, and politely excused herself. Ten minutes later she was lying in bed wondering why adults found it so easy to fool themselves.

Chapter Seven

Judith checked the paper one last time to be absolutely certain she had the right address before stepping forward and ringing the doorbell of her first house of call. The door was opened by an elderly man who welcomed her in with a heartfelt handshake. He waited politely until she'd hung up her coat before handing her a piece of paper explaining that it was a list with instructions his wife had left for her to do. Judith thought it rather long considering she was only supposed to be there for one and a half hours, but withheld from commenting and simply asked him where they kept their cleaning supplies, and within minutes she was hard at work.

It had taken her just over an hour to complete the list for downstairs. She'd cleaned all the windows, she'd dusted and vacuumed all the rooms, had cleaned the downstairs toilet and was making her way up the stairs to start on the bathroom when an elderly woman walked in through the front door. Judith stopped her ascent and headed back down the stairs to introduce herself. The woman gave her a quick glance over before loosely accepting her handshake. "Have you been following my instructions?"

Judith was taken aback by the woman's directness and simply replied, "Yes."

"Show me."

Judith didn't like the manner in which she was being spoken to and for a moment considered saying something, but despite her feelings she surprised herself by walking back into the living room and pointing out what she'd done. Then, Judith watched in disbelief as the woman started to inspect the windows, exaggeratedly scrutinizing them up close. "Did you use spiritus?"

"Yes, just like you wrote on the list."

"It doesn't look like you have."

Judith didn't know whether to laugh at the absurdity of the remark or feel insulted.

"I can assure you I have."

"Do it again."

Judith couldn't believe she was being told to clean a window she had only just cleaned.

"And I can assure you, I will be calling the agency about you."

Before Judith could respond the woman turned and left the room leaving Judith staring after her dumbstruck. She wanted to stick up for herself, but wasn't quite sure how to and at the same time didn't want to cause trouble. She needed the work and couldn't risk losing it over her pride or the quirks of a rude old lady. She made a noble attempt at putting her feelings of indignation and disbelief to one side and started cleaning the window again.

❖

Judith felt completely done in and struggled to keep up with Emily's chatter. She had managed to pick her up from school on time and was grateful to be finally sitting, albeit on the streetcar. She had never been someone to cower from hard work, but there was a limit to how many windows a person could clean in one day. Fortunately her other clients had not been like her first. They had been polite and had seemed grateful for her work. She had especially enjoyed her visit to Miss Rossum. The old woman had seemed excited at her arrival and had welcomed her in enthusiastically. Miss Rossum had wanted them to work together, explaining that she liked to do things for herself and only wanted Judith to do the things she could not. So while Judith cleaned the windows and wiped away the cobwebs from the ceiling, Miss Rossum dusted her silver. While they worked, Miss Rossum talked about some of her experiences from during the Second World War and Judith listened intently. She'd been disappointed when the time had come to move on to her next client, but being reminded of what some people had had to endure during the war made her own problems seem less insurmountable, and she had left the old woman's house with a new sense of determination.

❖

When they entered the apartment they were greeted by the sound of classical music. Listening to it reminded Judith of her childhood, when she would be lying in her bed and would hear the faint sound of classical music. It meant her father was home and resting in his study. She would creep out of bed and quietly make her way along the hall and down the grand stairwell toward her father's study. She would find him sitting in his big old leather chair behind his big wooden desk with his head resting back, his tie undone, seemingly asleep. She would quietly but quickly cross the room, climb onto his lap, and cuddle up to his warm chest. Without a word he would raise his arms and engulf her. They would sit like that, warm and snug, surrounded by classical music, until she fell asleep. The next time she opened her eyes it would be morning and she'd be back in her bed as if she had never left it.

The memory warmed her, and while Emily rushed to the living room to put the TV on, Judith followed the music coming from Lizzy's study. The door was open and she could see Lizzy sitting at her desk leaning over a very thick manuscript. Her study wasn't messy, but it certainly looked chaotic. It was obvious that the room had been decorated with the same elegance as the rest of the apartment, but it was now overtaken by the paper, books, and tapes strewn about the room. Judith had no doubt that Lizzy knew where everything was, but she knew it would be a tall order for anyone else to find something without instructions and possibly the use of a compass.

She realized that this was the first time she was seeing Lizzy doing something other than eating or coming and going and allowed herself a moment to observe her unawares. She had only ever seen Lizzy wearing polo shirts or turtlenecks with either jeans or corduroy trousers, and today was no different. She was wearing a navy blue polo shirt with jeans. She was leaning over the manuscript, her head slightly tilted to the left resting in her hand, her fingers intertwined in her thick blond hair. In her other hand she held a red pen and was slowly following the lines on the page. Judith had already thought her a handsome woman, but the afternoon sun accentuated her delicate features, highlighting the soft curves of her cheeks, jaw, and slender neck.

She gently knocked on the door.

Lizzy's head snapped up and she stared at Judith with hazed blue eyes. She blinked several times and seemed confused. A trace of anguish swept across her features and she shook her head as if trying to vanquish an unwanted image or thought. "I...I must have lost track of time."

"Are you okay?"

"Yes." Lizzy stood abruptly and placed the manuscript in a drawer off to the side. She then paused, exhaling slowly before turning to face Judith again.

"So how did it go today?"

Judith was momentarily taken back by Lizzy's swift change of demeanor. She had no idea what had upset Lizzy, but in a matter of seconds she had completely found her composure again. Judith realized in that instant that Lizzy was very good at hiding her true emotions. "It was okay, can't complain. Are you sure you're okay?"

"I'm sure." She smiled as if to prove her point. "I thought I'd cook tonight, give you a break."

Judith was touched by the offer, but Lizzy had already done enough for them.

"It's nice of you to offer, but I'm fine."

"Going into people's homes to clean can be physically very hard work and can be mentally draining. I'm sure you could complain if you wanted to."

"No really, it wasn't that bad. Although I'm looking forward to having a shower and putting some clean clothes on."

"Well, there you go, then. It's settled. I'm cooking."

❖

Lizzy stepped out onto the terrace. The image of Maurice standing in her doorway still crowded her mind. She had been so consumed with her reading that for a brief moment she had lost touch with the here and now. It had been a long time since she had lost herself in her work like that. In the past she would frequently lose track of time and then look up to find Maurice already home, smiling at her from the doorway. When she heard the knock, her spirit had instantly lifted and she had automatically looked up expecting to see Maurice. Then in a split second, reality had catapulted itself through her consciousness, and it had cost her an enormous amount of mental effort not to crumble. Before today she would have, but even through her confusion, she had recognized the tiredness in Judith's face. The sudden concern she had felt for her had somehow helped her to compose herself again. She felt frustrated that she had confused the two very different women and felt immensely defeated at once again having to acknowledge the fact that Maurice would never again stand in her doorway.

From somewhere behind her Emily giggled at a cartoon. The innocent vivacious sound of a child resonating within her own home reasserted how different her life now was, but it also reminded her she was supposed to be cooking dinner. She stepped back inside, grateful to have something to occupy her mind.

She had already decided, earlier in the day, on cooking a chicken dish she used to make regularly. It was a dish that had what she considered to be a divine combination between sweet and hot. She knew that she would have to skip the hot part for Emily's sake.

She had already marinated the meat and had just finished

topping and tailing the beans when Judith entered the living room wearing a baggy pair of blue sweatpants and top with her wet hair combed back. She gave Emily a kiss on the top of her head before sitting at the kitchen counter.

"Do you want some help?"

"No. I'm fine."

"Are you sure?"

"Absolutely, you've cooked for me every night. It's only fair I cook you at least one edible meal."

"And how much of a health hazard am I exposing my daughter to?"

Lizzy laughed, releasing some of the tension she felt between her shoulders. "Well, I learned a long time ago that arsenic isn't the same as a parsnip."

"I should hope so. Are you sure I can't help?"

Lizzy liked the way Judith's eyes seemed to shine more brightly. "Absolutely."

"I suppose I could get on with some washing."

"Or you could just sit and relax."

"I suppose I could do that too."

Lizzy playfully ushered her away with a hand gesture. "Go on, get out of here. You're cluttering up my kitchen."

Judith laughed, but she did as she was told.

It had been a long time since Lizzy had last cooked a proper meal and as she threw the chicken into the wok she became aware of how much she was enjoying it. She used to cook this particular meal regularly, but had stopped when there hadn't been anyone to cook for anymore. She knew the last time she'd cooked this dish she had eaten it with Maurice, but couldn't remember when that was. Had it been a Tuesday like today or some other day of the week? Not being able to recall, not knowing, sickened her. She heard a movement behind her and looked over her shoulder. Emily had climbed onto one of the stools and was leaning over the counter, trying to see what Lizzy was cooking.

"Are you hungry?"

"Yes."

Lizzy remembered how she used to hate having to wait for her dinner when she was a kid and empathized with Emily. "Just another ten minutes."

"Shall I lay the table?"

"That would be a big help."

Emily climbed off the stool and went straight to the cupboard where the heat mats were kept. It felt strange to Lizzy to think that this young girl would know where that kind of stuff was in her home. The past, which had once been the present, was so different from the now, and for the last three years she had not wanted to accept this difference, but watching Emily stretch to place the heat mats on the dinner table was more irrefutable proof. She had never been able to rationalize the loss of Maurice and she still couldn't.

Dinner went smoothly. Everybody enjoyed the meal and the conversation was light and easy. Emily talked about school, Judith talked about her day, and Lizzy answered their questions about her day. Although she participated in the conversation and enjoyed their company, she felt shrouded in a sort of mist the whole time. She was aware that she was in the middle of this peaceful, homey, vibrant picture and yet she was separated from it by a vast, invisible void.

When the plates were empty and Judith started talking to Emily about her homework, Lizzy set about clearing the table and washing the dishes. She tried to imagine what it would have been like if she had let Maurice have the child she had always wanted. Instead of being alone she would still have a part of Maurice, but she also wondered if she would have been able to cope looking at that child every day, seeing the touch of Maurice in her, reminding her even more of her loss.

"A penny for your thoughts?"

Lizzy was surprised to find Judith standing next to her with a dish towel in one hand and a cup in the other. She had been so lost in her thoughts she hadn't noticed her.

"Oh, sorry, I was just thinking of work."

"How's it going?"

"Good. The storyboard's about finished and if all goes well we hope to start shooting in about six weeks' time."

"And do you film on, like"—Judith hesitated—"a real set?"

Lizzy smiled at the question. She was used to people having difficulty envisioning what making a movie entailed. The only thing they had to go on was what they saw on TV, the so-called behind-the-scenes interviews and such, and although a lot of movies were done by the big production companies using big studios and special effects, many movies were done by smaller companies and independent moviemakers. Even the big moviemakers had to improvise now and again.

"Well, there's no Hollywood studio involved if that's what you mean, but we have our locations, where there are actors acting, cameramen filming, and the like. You'll have to come one of the days."

"I'd like that."

Just then Emily walked into the kitchen. "Mommy, can we go to the park tomorrow?"

Judith clasped her hand to her mouth and Lizzy guessed straightaway what the problem was. Tomorrow was Wednesday, and in the Netherlands every elementary school kid had Wednesday afternoons free. Judith was supposed to work tomorrow, and it was way too late to call the agency. Lizzy knew there was only one solution.

"If you want I could pick her up."

Judith turned abruptly to face her, incredulously. "I couldn't ask that of you."

"It wouldn't be a problem. I'll leave Sam's early and do some work at home. That's if Emily doesn't mind."

Judith quickly explained to Emily what the problem was and Emily easily agreed to being picked up by Lizzy.

Judith turned to Lizzy again. "Are you sure it's not too much of a hassle?"

"Yes, it will be fine. Just tell me where the school is and I'll pick her up at twelve."

Judith lowered her head. "I have no idea how I'm ever going to repay you for your kindness."

Lizzy shrugged. "It's no big deal."

Judith placed a tentative hand on her arm. "It's a big deal to me."

The intensity with which Judith had spoken and the softness of her touch made the black hole in Lizzy's chest stir, and panic started to consume her.

"Yes, of course. Look, I forgot, I need to pop out for a bit."

Judith could do nothing but stare after her as Lizzy left the room and then the apartment. She had no idea what had just happened except that Lizzy had turned very pale and had fled, and all she had done was try to express her gratitude.

❖

Lizzy sat inside the dark interior of her car. She wasn't exactly sure where she was. She'd just gotten in her car and had headed for the highway and had driven for a few hours until she'd finally pulled over, not wanting to go back or go on. She looked out at the black sky and listened to the loud roar of silence occupying the space around her, the only thing louder being the sound of her own breathing reminding her over and over again of her loss. She rested her head on the steering wheel wanting desperately to scream at someone or something, to blame them, to dare them to take her too, but at the same time she struggled desperately not to. She had no right to want such a thing; she had made her promise. Guilt ricocheted through her being. Maurice had never had the choice—why should she? The black hole within her churned vigorously, her anger rising to the surface. She fought desperately to keep it in, fearing that if it escaped it would consume her.

After a while she leaned back in her seat again feeling exhausted and empty, but she had succeeded once again in achieving a blessed numbness. She had managed to lock her anger and frustration away in that deep hidden alcove that had scarred itself a niche in her soul, and with her true feelings now muted her mind was clear again. She had said that she would pick Emily up from school tomorrow, and to do that she would have to go back.

It was already late by the time Judith finally decided to go to bed. She'd expressly waited up in the hope of speaking to Lizzy. She had no idea what had gone wrong this evening, but the look of despondency in Lizzy's eyes when she had left had been unsettling. She felt concerned and wanted to see her back home safe, but she couldn't wait any longer; she had to be up early and she couldn't risk being late for work. She tried to write a note, but couldn't think of what to say and decided it best not to say anything.

As she curled up beneath the cold sheets she decided she would try to pay more attention to Lizzy's gestures and her state of mind. She wanted to understand what triggered her to shut down so abruptly and flee—so that she could avoid causing it, if nothing else.

Chapter Eight

Lizzy rang Sam's doorbell at nine the next morning. She was just about to give up waiting when a small-eyed, ruffled-looking Sam opened the door.

"Oh God, Lizzy, I'm so sorry. I never heard the alarm go off."

Although slightly annoyed, Lizzy couldn't help but forgive him. Sam was only wearing a T-shirt and a pair of underwear, and his spindly legs and lack of modesty were too comical for her to stay annoyed at him.

"Don't worry about it."

He stepped aside to let her in while rubbing the sleep out of his eyes.

"I had one of my inspired moments late last night and didn't get to bed until four this morning."

Lizzy felt no need to tell him that she had only managed a few hours' sleep herself. "I'm intrigued."

"I know we haven't discussed it, but I'm sure you're gonna love the change I've made."

"Well, in that case I forgive you for leaving me out on the doorstep. Now go get dressed and I'll make us some coffee. Oh, and by the way, I have to cut it short today. I have to be somewhere at twelve."

"Well, I'll forgive *you* if you like my adaptation."

"Move it."

"I'm already on my way."

Lizzy turned away at the sight of his wiry legs disappearing up the stairs and made her way toward his kitchen. She knew where everything was due to the many late nights of working on prior projects with Sam, and soon the house was filled with the scent of percolated coffee. Fifteen minutes later they were both seated at Sam's drawing table going through the latest adaptations to the storyboard. Lizzy was impressed with the changes he had made during the night. He had managed to capture the essence of an emotion she wanted in a particular scene. Lizzy always knew where she wanted the camera and what the picture should look like. The whole movie would play itself out in her head like an internal cinema; the storyboard was more of a reminder for her as well as a visual guideline for the rest of the crew. But her internal cinema had been suffering for a long time now. She'd reach a scene in her head knowing what she wanted from it, but she couldn't quite visualize it and struggled to bring out the emotional intensity she usually quite easily pulled out from each scene. Sam's uncanny ability to understand and draw what she pictured in her head was proving more valuable than ever before.

They soon lost themselves in their work and it was only when Sam started to yawn and stretch his muscles that Lizzy happened to glance at her watch.

"Shit, I'm gonna be late."

"So what's so important you have to dump me halfway through the day?"

Lizzy pulled on her jacket. "I have to pick up...someone at twelve." She almost said *a child*, but thought better of it. It would only mean a load of questions she didn't have time to answer.

Sam wriggled his eyebrows. "Anyone important?"

"Yeah, Steven Spielberg's asked for a private lesson on camera work."

Before Sam had a chance to retort, Lizzy was already out the front door. She managed to get to the school with five minutes to spare and was lucky enough to find a place for the car. She then joined the other adults who were lingering just inside the school gate. She felt out of place among them. With few exceptions, they seemed relaxed and gave the impression they knew exactly what they were doing. Lizzy couldn't help but wonder how many of them secretly felt inadequate.

A bell rang from somewhere inside the school building and a flood of kids came spilling through the doors onto the opposite side of the playground. Lizzy scanned the crowd of little people until she spotted Emily. She noticed straightaway that she didn't look as cheerful as she usually did. Emily spotted her too and after a quick good-bye to her friends joined Lizzy at the gates and together they set off down the street in the direction of the car. Lizzy wasn't sure what to say to Emily and felt it best to go for the obvious.

"So how was school today?"

"Good. I got an invitation to a party."

"Did you? That's cool."

Lizzy opened the car door for her and waited until Emily had fastened her seat belt before closing the door and getting in herself. After safely reaching the end of the street without running over any parents or their kids, Lizzy turned her attention back to Emily.

"So when's the party?"

"Next week Friday. It's not really a party. It's a sleepover."

"That's just as good, isn't it?" Lizzy remembered her first sleepover and how much she had enjoyed sleeping in a bed with two other girls. She had just turned ten and realized that girls were a great replacement for teddy bears. "Better, if I recall correctly."

"Mm-hmm."

Lizzy glanced at her through the rearview mirror. "You don't sound too cheerful about it."

Emily frowned, but didn't respond.

"Come on, spill the beans."

Emily's frown turned into a quizzical smile. "Spill the beans?"

"Yeah, you know, cough it up, throw it in the group, tell me why it's only all right."

"It's not the party, it's Mrs. Bouwman." Emily had said the name with a slight tone of annoyance.

Lizzy had no idea who Mrs. Bouwman was.

"Is she your teacher?"

"Yes."

"Okay, so what has Mrs. Bouwman done?"

Emily let out a long sigh. "She told us that we're going to do a school play about Peter Pan and Captain Hook."

Lizzy still didn't see what the problem was.

"Well, a school play sounds like fun."

Emily frowned. "It is, and anybody who wants to can audition for a part in it."

Lizzy wondered what she was missing. She still didn't understand what was wrong.

"Do you want to audition?"

"Yes, but when I asked Mrs. Bouwman if I could audition to be a pirate, she said that pirates were always boys and that it wouldn't be historically correct and that I would be much happier in a different role."

Lizzy wondered if this Mrs. Bouwman was teaching the right grade. Who cared what was historically correct at the age of seven, and besides, wasn't Peter Pan fiction? She didn't like to see Emily so down, and before she knew what she was doing she was already speaking.

"I'll tell you what, as soon as we get back home we'll make you a pirate costume and then you can practice being a pirate and then when it's time for you to audition you just do the pirate thing instead."

Emily's face was stern. "I don't think Mrs. Bouwman will allow it."

"Well, you'll just have to prove her wrong, won't you? Everybody should be given a fair chance, and if someone denies you yours, then you have to fight for it. If you still don't get to be a pirate, well, at least you tried."

Lizzy watched in the rearview mirror as a cheeky smile slowly spread across Emily's face.

As soon as they got home they set about making a pirate

costume. Lizzy dug out an old pair of trousers and cut them so that they reached just above Emily's knees. She had to make an extra hole in her belt to keep the too-wide trousers from falling down, but all in all, the bagginess only helped to make Emily look more authentic. They cut out swords from cardboard, made eye patches from black paper and string, and in no time were jumping about the living room playing pirates, using the couches as makeshift ships.

❖

"Do you surrender, young pirate of the seas?"

Emily breathed hard, her stare strong and determined as she glared up at the enemy whose sword was pointed at her chest. *"Never!"*

Emily jumped to her feet and started attacking her enemy again with all her might.

"Ahem!"

Both pirates stopped in midair, panting, their swords raised.

"Mommy!" Emily jumped off her ship and ran up to Judith. "We're playing pirates, Mommy. Do you want to play?"

Judith hugged her before sitting down on the couch Emily had just jumped from. Lizzy could tell she was tired. "Pirates, eh?"

"Yes, for the school play."

"What school play?"

"Peter Pan!"

Lizzy took off her eye patch and made her way to the kitchen as Judith patiently listened to Emily tell her about the play and what Mrs. Bouwman had said and what she and Lizzy had planned. Only once did Judith look Lizzy's way, and it dawned on her that she might have crossed a line.

"Do you want to play? You can be Tinker Bell, kidnapped by the pirates."

"Maybe some other time. I think you'd better get changed. You've got your art class, remember?"

"Okay, Mommy. Maybe later?"

Judith smiled and stroked Emily's face. "Maybe. Now go and get changed."

As Emily ran out of the room, an awkward silence filled the air.

"I was worried about you last night."

Lizzy was surprised. She'd planned on apologizing to Judith about the way she had abruptly left last night, but she hadn't expected her to worry about her.

"Yes, I wanted to apologize for leaving like that."

"Why did you?"

Lizzy had no idea how to answer her truthfully. How on earth could she explain how she had felt? At the same time she didn't want to lie to her. She felt her heart sink lower as no appropriate answer came to mind.

"I didn't mean to upset you last night, Judith, and I'm sorry if I crossed a line today with Emily. I didn't stop to think that you might not agree. Otherwise I would never have encouraged her like this." Lizzy knew she wasn't answering the question, but this was the best she could do.

Judith didn't respond straight away and Lizzy felt even more uncomfortable under her gaze, but she hoped Judith would accept her apology and let the matter of last night rest.

"It's all right. I don't know if I would have encouraged Emily to do this"—she picked up the sword Emily had left in her lap—"but I also don't like people telling my girl there's something she can't do. That Mrs. Bouwman is a nice person and a good teacher as well, but her views on women are somewhat misplaced in this modern day." She gave a quick wave of the sword. "And besides, I quite like the idea of being a pirate myself."

❖

Lizzy lay restless in bed as her mind mulled over the events of the past few days. She did not regret offering Judith and Emily a safe place to stay, but their presence triggered memories of her life with Maurice—memories she didn't want to be reminded of, because they made continuing on without her impossible. Little things they said or did would unintentionally unleash the pain and anger she tried hard to keep buried.

Last night she had barely been able to cope with her grief, and the weight of life itself had seemed too heavy to bear, but this afternoon she had played pirates with Emily and had thoroughly enjoyed herself. The contradiction was confusing. She thought about Judith, a devoted mother, tired, but patient: a mother who wanted the best for her child, but going without it herself. She wondered whether Maurice would have agreed with her approach to the pirate issue. She couldn't believe she had been so stubborn. She would have given Maurice anything she wanted, except the thing she wanted most. She had always known that Maurice would have been a great mother, but she'd been convinced that she herself wouldn't. The idea of bringing up a child had seemed too daunting, and although she still felt that way, she couldn't believe she had let her fears get the better of her. She turned to face Maurice's side of the bed, imagining her there, beside her, sleeping softly. She remembered the softness of her lips and the gentleness of her touch. Their absence burned her skin. Their lovemaking had sometimes been spontaneous and quick, the urgency too much, but mostly it had been intensely intimate and deeply passionate. She squeezed her eyes shut, trying to block out the memory and calm the familiar consuming ache inside her. No matter how hard she tried, she couldn't stop missing her.

Chapter Nine

Lizzy had slept poorly. Visions of Judith and Maurice had consumed her dreams, their faces mixing together to form the face of a child. She'd awoken feeling exhausted and hadn't felt up to seeing anyone, so she'd made a few quick phone calls to rearrange her appointments, then settled down in her study to work, hoping to banish the echoing whispers of her dreams.

It was late afternoon when her concentration was abruptly disturbed by the ringing of the phone next to her desk. Trying to keep the annoyance out of her voice, she took the call. "Lizzy speaking."

"Could I speak to Miss Judith Hilford please?"

"Judith isn't here at the moment..." Lizzy glanced at her watch and saw it was nearly five o'clock. "But she should be back at any moment. Can I pass on a message?"

"Yes, could you tell her Yvonne from Top Line has called and that we have more work available? It's evening work from five to eight starting Monday, and to call me before ten tomorrow if she wants it?"

"Sure. I'll tell her as soon as she gets in."

Lizzy knew that Judith wanted more hours and that this was supposed to be good news, but a part of her wished that Judith didn't have to do this work and that she could go back to teaching, where her heart lay.

It was half past five when Judith and Emily returned, and she went to greet them.

"Lizzy!" Emily's face was full of delight. "Can we play pirates later? Please, please?"

"Emily!" Judith's tone was more cautionary than a rebuff.

Lizzy enjoyed seeing the sparkle in Emily's eyes and couldn't help herself. "If your mom says it's okay."

Emily looked up at Judith expectantly and Judith gently patted the top of her head. "First your homework."

"Yippee! Thanks, Mom, thanks, Lizzy." She skipped down the hall toward her bedroom.

Lizzy turned to Judith. "The agency called while you were out."

Judith stopped unbuttoning her coat, her expression hopeful. Lizzy knew Judith was hoping for a teaching position and wished she could tell her what she wanted to hear, but instead relayed the message as she had been given it.

Judith's expression turned sullen as soon as Lizzy mentioned the hours they were offering her. She finished unbuttoning her coat, hung it up, and pushed some loose strands of hair behind her ears before responding. "I can't do late-afternoon work. I've got a child to look after. I told them that when I signed up."

Although Judith's tone was neutral, Lizzy picked up on her frustration. She appreciated that being a single parent wasn't easy and understood how much Judith wanted to make things right for Emily. She wanted to say something encouraging, but knew it would only sound flimsy under the circumstance.

"I'm sorry, Lizzy. I don't mean to sound ungrateful, because I am grateful for what they've done for me so far. It's just—"

"I understand, and you have every right to feel frustrated. What you're trying to do isn't easy."

Judith tilted her head slightly and spoke tenderly. "You're very attentive to other people's feelings, aren't you?"

Judith's remark made Lizzy feel very uneasy and she wished she was back in the sanctuary of her study. She tried to sound as casual as she could. "No more than anybody else." She rubbed the back of her neck. "Anyway, I have to get back to work." Judith nodded and Lizzy turned and left her alone in the hall. She felt like a jerk for leaving her like that, but she just couldn't cope with dealing with that kind of scrutiny.

She tried to concentrate on her work again, but thoughts of Judith's predicament kept creeping in. She knew Judith needed money if she was to support herself and this evening work would give her that extra she needed, but she couldn't do that and look after Emily at the same time. Lizzy pushed back in her chair, annoyed at herself. She could easily make it home for the afternoons to babysit Emily—at least until they started shooting, and that wouldn't be for another good few weeks. So why wasn't she offering to help? She shook her head, frustrated. She wasn't offering because she was afraid of getting even more involved with them than she already was, and she was scared she wouldn't be able to handle any more. Cussing at herself, she stood and headed toward the living room.

Judith was seated on one of the couches with a steaming mug in her hand. She looked haggard and was staring out in front of her lost in thought. Lizzy sat on the opposite couch and took a deep breath.

"If you want, I could make it back for the afternoons and keep an eye on Emily for you, at least for the next few weeks."

"I know you mean well, Lizzy, but I couldn't let you do that."

"It wouldn't be a problem. I'd only have to make a few phone calls and rearrange a few things, but—"

"There's more to looking after a child than just keeping an eye on her, Lizzy. She would need to be fed, her homework checked, tucked into bed. I mean, have you ever taken care of a child before? And I'm not talking about playing pirates for an afternoon."

Judith's question hit home and Lizzy felt a wave of guilt toward Maurice sweep over her. Her chest immediately started churning and she did her best to respond calmly.

"No. I haven't, but I wasn't offering to be her mother when you weren't around. I just simply meant you could go and work the evening shift if you wanted, knowing that your daughter would at least be safe." With every word her chest grew heavier and she stood. "I would never presume to know what being a parent is about, and I certainly would not presume to be able to fulfill the task."

She strode out of the room and headed straight for her study, wishing she had never offered her help in the first place. She needed things to be simple. She couldn't go on if things weren't kept simple.

❖

Judith walked down the hall to her bedroom, consciously aware that she was passing Lizzy's study. Her legs felt heavy as well as her heart. She hadn't meant to be so rough on her. She knew Lizzy meant well, but the idea of needing someone's help to look after Emily only enforced the reality that she couldn't do this alone. She was doing her best, but somehow it just didn't seem to be enough. She also knew that she would have to contact Menno soon, and that weighed heavily on her mind. She thought back to her life only a few weeks ago. It seemed so strange now, like a distant dream, but she hadn't dreamed it. It had been her reality for years. When had it started to go wrong? Had it ever really been right? If her father were alive, what would he think of her now?

She slowly undressed and pulled on some comfortable clothing. She would have preferred going to bed, but she still had dinner to cook and Emily's homework to check. As she retied her hair she thought about Lizzy and her incredible offer. It seemed as if Lizzy was always either offering her support or backing away from her. Judith had felt too tired to take her proposal seriously, but there was something about the way Lizzy had responded to her that made her think nothing Lizzy did or said was without weight. Although quick to avoid anything that could be considered personal, Lizzy was certainly not superficial.

❖

A soft knock on her door caused Lizzy to look up. Emily was hovering just inside the doorway already dressed in her homemade pirate costume. Lizzy wasn't in the mood for playing anymore, but Emily's face shone bright with excitement and Lizzy didn't have the heart to disappoint her.

"Aha! I take it your homework's finished, then?"

Emily's eyes were big as saucers as she nodded.

"Well then, let me just put this away…" Lizzy picked up a piece of paper and placed it inside a drawer, but it was the same drawer she had put her own cardboard sword in. With one swift movement, she grabbed her sword, turned, and shouted playfully, "En garde!"

Emily let out a squeal and then stabbed the air with her own sword. They battled up and down the hall, taking turns being slaughtered only to rise with a sudden burst of energy to fight the enemy again. One would be on the ground with a sword pointed at her chest while the other demanded, "Surrender or die." To which the other would shout, "Never!" and the attack would commence.

Lizzy was enjoying herself, but was relieved when Judith called Emily for dinner. Panting, she stepped back.

"I thinks the captain be wantin' ya in 'er cabin."

Emily's face was red from all of the running around and her eyes sparkled. "I'm a pirate. I don't have to do anything I don't want to."

Lizzy approached her slowly, lowering her voice in an attempt to sound menacing.

"Aye, but that's where ya wrong. A pirate must always do what 'er captain tells 'er to do, or else…" Lizzy pretended to look sideways as if making sure no one was listening. "Ya'll be made to walk the plank."

Emily's expression was challenging, but Lizzy could tell she was trying to work it out. "What's that?"

"Aye, that's somethin' every pirate dreads, but I'll tell ya's about it after ya've been to see ya captain."

Emily's expression turned defiant. "Tell me now."

Lizzy stepped aside and put a finger to her mouth and whispered, "Later. Now go before the captain catches us speakin'."

Emily stood for a moment longer, then put a finger to her own mouth and whispered back, "Later."

Lizzy marveled at Emily's indefatigable energy as she watched her run down the hall toward the living room. She headed back to her study and was in the process of placing her sword back in its drawer when there was another gentle knock at her door. She turned expecting to see Emily again, but was surprised to find Judith standing there.

"This captain wants to be knowin' whether this pirate will be a comin' to dinner or not?"

Lizzy hadn't expected the invitation, not after what had transpired between them earlier, and she felt uncomfortable with the idea of sitting with them at the table. She opened her mouth to decline, but Judith quickly continued, no longer playful.

"I'd like it if you did."

She said it so meaningfully that Lizzy realized Judith regretted what had happened just as much as she did, and this was her way of making things right between them again. Judith's initiative deserved willingness and Lizzy knew she had to accept.

The night air was nippy, but Lizzy ignored the discomfort, concentrating instead on lighting up her cigarette. She knew that Maurice would strongly disapprove and she tried to imagine what she would say if she caught her out there. The bay door behind her slid open and Judith stepped onto the terrace. She was in her pajamas but had a shawl wrapped around her shoulders.

"May I join you?"

Lizzy would have preferred to be alone, but couldn't find it in herself to say so. "Sure."

Judith closed the door behind her before joining Lizzy at the railing. "Those things could kill you, you know."

Lizzy flicked the ash of her cigarette. "Yep, so could a million other things."

A few moments passed while they both stared into the clouded night sky. They hadn't yet talked about what had happened between them earlier, and even though she would prefer to leave it that way, Lizzy guessed that Judith had come out there just for that reason. After dinner she had retreated back to her study in the hope of losing herself in her work again, but she hadn't been able to concentrate. She felt stupid for having offered to look after Emily and couldn't ignore the lingering feeling of remorse she felt toward Maurice. She had stayed in her study until she knew Judith had gone to bed. Only then did she decide to call it quits for the night, thinking it would be safe to come out and enjoy a private smoke before going to bed.

"I'm sorry about what I said earlier. I was feeling tired and frustrated and I let that out on you. It was unfair of me to do so."

Lizzy managed a slight smile. "Don't worry about it. You were right anyway. I have no idea what it takes to look after a child. It was a stupid idea."

Judith was quick to continue. "Please don't say that. I didn't mean what I said. I'm sure you'd make a great parent, and it wasn't a stupid idea. It was an extremely kind offer." Judith turned to face her. "I think that's my problem."

"How do you mean?"

"It's just, well, I don't know anyone who would have been as kind to us as you have and still seem prepared to do more for us, and it's making me feel even more awkward than I already do. I guess I need to understand why you're doing this."

"It's no big deal, Judith."

"You keep saying that."

"Well, it isn't."

"If it's no big deal, then why do you try to avoid talking about it?"

Lizzy rubbed her left temple that had started throbbing. "Please don't do this."

"Do what?"

"Make things complicated."

"How am I making things complicated?" Judith sounded confused.

Lizzy didn't respond and Judith continued in a gentle voice. "What happens to you at these moments?"

Lizzy's stomach lurched and for a moment she thought she was going to throw up. She tightened her grip on the railing. "Nothing, just leave it, will you?"

"Is it because of me?"

"No. It's got nothing to do with you."

"Is it because of us being here?"

Lizzy spun around. "Does there have to be a reason for everything?"

Judith didn't reply, merely looked back at her with a mixture of confusion and compassion. Lizzy quickly turned away and headed indoors, but stopped and took a deep breath before turning back to face Judith.

"I know how hard it is to accept help, believe me…" Lizzy swallowed hard. "Because it only proves to you that you need it. I've offered you my help because I knew it was the right thing to do, and that's all there is to it. It really is as simple as that, for me anyway. Why can't you just accept that?"

"Because nothing is ever that simple, Lizzy."

"Exactly. Life is complicated enough, so what's wrong with *trying* to keep things simple if it helps you get by?"

"Because the type of simplicity you're implying is unrealistic."

"Well, it's the only way I know how to cope with reality." Lizzy's voice nearly broke and she turned abruptly and left the terrace.

Judith turned back to face the night sky. Her heart was racing and she felt terrible.

She'd come out to apologize and somehow she'd gone and made it worse. She wiped a tear away. Maybe Lizzy was right. Maybe the best way to cope was to keep it all as simple as possible. She shivered in the night air and pulled the shawl tighter around her shoulders, wishing she didn't feel so alone.

CHAPTER TEN

L izzy found herself walking down a long, dark tunnel. She couldn't see where she was going and reached out, feeling cold, damp stones. She wasn't scared, but she was acutely aware of an overwhelming sense of urgency. Suddenly the floor gave way and she was falling, faster and faster down a black shaft. She relaxed and waited to smash into the ground, but the inevitable collision never happened. Instead she just kept falling. Windows appeared in the wall of the shaft and behind each one stood Maurice, watching her fall, looking immensely sad. Lizzy knew she was the cause of her sadness and tried to reach out to her, but as she did so she understood why Maurice was sad. She was sad because Lizzy didn't care that she was falling. Then she had the overwhelming feeling that there was something she was supposed to be doing, but she had no idea what. As she tried to figure out what, her fall slowed until her feet gently touched the floor.

Lizzy turned onto her back and groaned. Her head was throbbing and her mouth was dry. She slowly opened her eyes, letting them adjust to the light coming through the window. She could hear noise in the distance and figured Emily was up watching a cartoon. She remembered her conversation with Judith on the terrace and quickly pulled the sheet over her head, cringing. She hadn't meant to be so abrupt, or weak, but somehow things had gotten the better of her.

She curled up under the sheets, telling herself that if she just stayed in bed she could pretend everything was okay and she wouldn't have to face Judith. Then she let out a slow growl. She knew she couldn't hide there all day. Hiding didn't solve things. She'd tried it before and it hadn't worked. She shoved back the sheets and forced herself to get up. She owed Judith an apology, and although she had no idea what to say, she knew she had to face the music.

❖

Judith was in the kitchen absentmindedly watching Emily as she watched her cartoons. She was thinking about the conversation or, better put, the exchange of words she had had with Lizzy last night. It had unnerved her and she'd slept poorly because of it.

One of the reasons she had left Menno was that he wouldn't allow her the freedom to decide things for herself. Now that she had that freedom, it scared the life out of her. Deciding to accept someone else's help, no matter how small or how big the offer, meant two things: one, that she had to make yet another important decision; and two, that she couldn't yet make it through life on her own, which only reinforced her feelings of inadequacy. Her need to understand Lizzy's motives was her way of trying to cope with these feelings and somehow make it easier to accept. She just didn't want to make things worse than they already were, and she didn't think it fair that another person should have to rearrange her life to accommodate hers. It was clear to her that something was going on with Lizzy. Something she didn't yet understand, and although Lizzy had denied it, Judith knew their presence had certainly triggered whatever it was, and she hated the idea that she was somehow responsible for any discomfort Lizzy might feel.

Her mind snapped back to the present when Lizzy entered the room. She looked as tired as Judith felt, and Judith guessed that Lizzy had had a bad night's sleep as well. She filled the kettle with water, wondering what she should say, but Lizzy spoke first.

"I owe you an apology."

Judith flipped the lid on the kettle shut and switched it on. "No, you don't."

"Yes, I do. I wasn't particularly nice to you last night."

Judith stared at the kettle. "I shouldn't have pushed you like that."

"You didn't push me to do anything. I...I went into defense mode and spoke without thinking."

Lizzy's humbleness was endearing and Judith turned to face her properly, sincerely wanting to understand her. "Why is that, Lizzy? Why do you go into defense mode?"

Lizzy rubbed the back of her neck as she struggled to answer. "I...I...Does it matter why?"

Judith was momentarily at a loss for words. In the instant that their eyes had locked, she had glimpsed that pain again. It had for the briefest of moments flickered bare before the very tangible barrier had shot up, hiding it from sight. She held Lizzy's defiant stare and realized that what Lizzy was carrying inside her was so painful she felt she needed to hide it from the world. Judith felt an enormous amount of affection for her.

"If something didn't matter, Lizzy, there would be no need in hiding from it."

Lizzy opened her mouth to speak, but then closed it again and started rubbing her left temple. She looked so lost that if Lizzy had been a child, Judith would have picked her up and comforted her. Instead she finished making her a cup of tea.

❖

Judith wiped bathwater out of her eyes while chiding herself for not having anticipated the shower. She was helping Emily bathe and had just told her that she was going to buy her a new winter coat in the morning. Emily's excitement had caused a cascade of water to fly up, half drenching Judith in the process. Earlier that morning, after dropping Emily off at school and with only a few moments to spare before her first cleaning assignment, she'd gone to the nearest

ATM and had excitedly punched in her new code to her new bank account. She had held her breath and crossed her fingers and prayed that her first week's pay was in. When she saw the numbers appear on the screen she had quickly clasped her mouth as relief cascaded through her body and soul. It wasn't much, but she would be able to give Lizzy some money, and more importantly, she would be able to get Emily the new coat she needed.

"I wish it was tomorrow already."

Judith helped Emily out of the bath and started drying her off. "Emily, you shouldn't wish your days away."

"Can I have a pink coat?"

Judith did her best to keep her dislike of the idea out of her voice. "Let's wait and see, shall we."

"Can we stop for a burger?"

"Maybe."

"Can Lizzy come?"

Judith hadn't expected that request and was surprised that Emily had asked. It had been ages since she had had some real quality time with Emily and she was looking forward to it.

She helped Emily into her pajamas. "I think Lizzy has more important things to do than go shopping with us, sweetheart."

"Can I ask her, please, Mommy?"

Judith didn't expect that Lizzy would like the idea of gallivanting around town for a kid's coat, especially after the way things had been going between them the last few days, but Emily was already scrambling to her feet. "Yippee! I'll go ask her straight away."

"Hold on, I never said…" But it was too late. She'd hesitated too long and now Emily had taken off. Judith remained seated on the edge of the bath trying to understand her feelings. On the one hand she was glad that Emily and Lizzy were getting along, but she also worried that Emily might be getting too attached to her. After all, she wasn't planning on staying here long. She could tell by the fast patter of Emily's feet coming back down the hall that her charm had gotten her what she wanted.

After finally getting Emily to settle down for the night, she decided to tackle the dishes before retiring to her own room, but was pleasantly surprised to find them done already. She started making herself a hot cup of chocolate when she heard keys in the front door. She hadn't noticed Lizzy leave and had just presumed she was still in her study. She had a flashback to the night when Lizzy had walked in unexpectedly and she cringed inwardly. Lizzy entered the living room and misinterpreted Judith's expression.

"Did I startle you?"

"No, no, I just hadn't noticed you'd left."

Lizzy lifted the DVD she was holding. "I fancied watching a movie."

"What's it about?"

"I don't know."

Judith was surprised by Lizzy's answer. "You rented a movie, but you don't know which one?"

"Yeah, well, it was hard choosing." Lizzy sounded shy. "I haven't rented a movie in a long time. In the past I watched so many it was hard finding one I hadn't seen. Now there are so many new movies I couldn't choose, so I just picked the one right in front of me. The boy at the counter said it was a good one, though."

Judith smiled at Lizzy's strange decision-making process.

Lizzy seemed to hesitate. "Do you want to watch it with me?"

Judith couldn't remember when she had last sat to watch a good movie, and the idea suddenly seemed very appealing.

"That depends. If you've picked a horror I'll have to skip it. I watched a movie about ghouls when I was fourteen and I still feel the urge to look under my bed."

"Yeah, you and half the world's population."

Judith enjoyed Lizzy's laughter. There was openness and honesty in it and she thought it a shame that Lizzy didn't laugh more often.

Two hours later the credits rolled up the screen and Judith turned to face Lizzy, who was sitting at the other end of the couch.

"Thank you. I enjoyed that."

"You're welcome." Lizzy stood and started to remove the

DVD and Judith remembered Emily's invitation to join them in the morning.

"About tomorrow, you don't have to come if you don't want to. I know how hard it is to deny a kid when they stand in front of you all sweet and eager."

"It's true I find it difficult to deny such a cute face and she did catch me off guard, but I gave her my word. Unless, of course, you want to be alone with her. I can understand you might want some time with just the two of you."

Judith marveled at Lizzy's attentiveness and felt a little childish for originally being opposed to her joining them.

"No, no, join us. Emily really wants you to come, and I'm going to need all the moral support I can get when it comes to choosing the color."

Lizzy raised her eyebrows and Judith smiled. "You'll find out soon enough tomorrow."

"If you want we could take my car. I have an inner-city parking permit. Saves a lot of hassle with public transport on a Saturday."

"Oh well, if there's a car service involved." Judith wriggled her eyebrows, pretending that solved the matter.

Lizzy laughed and Judith found herself looking forward to tomorrow again.

❖

Judith closed the door to the lady's restroom behind her and immediately recognized Emily's laughter among the noisy bustle of the café. The sound warmed her soul, but also panicked her. They'd already been hunting for a coat for a few hours before they had decided to stop and have a bite to eat, and Emily was just as excited as she had been when she'd woken that morning. Lizzy had been nothing but patient and attentive to Emily, but Judith was growing increasingly anxious that Lizzy would soon get irritated by Emily's constant chatter. As she approached their table she saw what was making Emily laugh. Lizzy was flipping a coaster from off the edge of the table and then catching it in midair. Emily's attempts at copying her meant the coaster kept shooting off in all directions. It was so clear that Emily was enjoying herself without fear of reprimand and Lizzy was helping create that feeling. The idea that somebody else besides herself could show such interest in Emily made her want to cry. She drew in a long breath and told herself to relax and just go with the flow.

The rest of the afternoon was spent going in and out of shops until Emily finally found a coat she insisted was exactly what she wanted. Judith struggled not to burst out laughing when she noticed Lizzy's expression as Emily reached for a bright pink coat, but also felt a surprising surge of warmth toward her when Emily came out of the cubicle asking her what she thought. Lizzy stated without hesitation and with convincing enthusiasm that she thought the coat looked great. Judith knew that Emily would probably outgrow it in a year's time and hoped she'd be done with the color pink by then.

By the time they got back Judith's feet were killing her and she was looking forward to relaxing with a nice cup of tea. While Emily dashed to the bathroom to look at herself in the mirror, Judith headed straight for kitchen to fill the kettle. She realized that Lizzy was watching her with a grin.

"What?"

"I'm having a bad influence on you." Lizzy nodded toward the kettle. "You haven't even taken your coat off and you're already making tea."

"It's the pink. It's scrambled my brains."

Lizzy rolled her eyes and smiled. "Yeah, I know what you mean, but she does look cute in it."

"Yeah, but then again, my girl looks cute in anything."

"Like mother, like daughter."

To Judith's horror she felt herself blush. Lizzy seemed to notice and stopped grinning and quickly changed the conversation. "How about I order us some pizza or something?"

Emily walked in just at that moment and squealed her opinion on the matter. "Pizza? Oh please, Mommy!"

"I could also pick up another movie if you like."

Judith did feel too tired to cook and she was still reveling in the casualness of the day, but she also knew it didn't really matter how she felt. She looked back and forth between the two of them and knew it was already a done deal.

Emily went with Lizzy to get the pizza and help pick out a movie and Judith stayed behind so she could change into something more comfortable and make a quick salad to go with the pizza. She thought back on the day. Despite her apprehension throughout the first part of it, she couldn't remember the last time she'd enjoyed herself so much. It had been great to spend a whole day with Emily and it had been great sharing it with Lizzy. To realize she had been holding her breath all morning waiting for the bubble to burst only reminded her why she had left Menno. She had unconsciously expected Lizzy to react like him, but she hadn't. At no point ever had she lost patience with Emily. She had been kind and supportive in an unobtrusive manner. Judith let her head fall back against the back of the couch and wondered how on earth she had become a woman who let her actions and feelings be dictated so finely by another person. She remembered Lizzy's words. *"Like mother, like daughter."* Did Lizzy really think she was cute? She felt her cheeks burn again.

Chapter Eleven

L izzy was just putting on her jacket when the phone rang.
"Hey, guess who's back? Did you miss me? You have
to come over and see the awesome things I've brought back with
me."

Lizzy could already imagine the large amount of completely
useless tourist jumble Chris would have spent his money on.

"I'm surprised that customs lets you back in the country every
time, considering all the junk you bring back."

"Just for that I'm going to give your gift to the neighbor."

"Yeah right, give her my best regards."

Chris snorted. "So are you coming over or what?"

"I can't. It's Wednesday. I've got to pick Emily up from school
and I promised to take her to Vondelpark."

"Emily?" Chris sounded surprised.

Lizzy kept quiet, waiting for the penny to drop.

"Oh, my God, Lizzy. I thought Judith would be long gone by
now. I was hoping she'd call me soon. So they're still at your place,
then?"

"Yep."

"And you're all right with that?"

"We're doing just fine, although our first introduction could
have gone more smoothly. Look, I'm glad you've enjoyed yourself
and that you got back safely, but I have to go or I'll be late."

"Wait, pick me up too and we can talk in the park. It's been ages since I last played on a swing."

"Be ready. I'm leaving now."

Before Chris had a chance to reply, she hung up and left.

❖

Chris clambered into the car wearing a large-brimmed hat that had corks hanging on strings all around its brim.

Lizzy shook her head. "You have to be kidding me."

Chris tried to look innocent. "What? The woman who sold it me said it made me look handsomely rugged."

"I have no doubt. I bet she had gold teeth as well."

Chris waved his hand in dismissal. "You're just jealous. So tell me, what's going on?"

Lizzy shifted gear and pulled away from the curb. "There's nothing to tell."

Chris looked at her incredulously. "What do you mean, there's nothing to tell? When I left you weren't picking up kids from school and taking them to the park."

"Hey, when I left I didn't have a woman and her child living in my place."

"Yeah, well, I gathered you wouldn't mind, and I knew they'd be gone by the time you got back."

"That's just it, I was only gone a few days."

Chris's eyes widened, then his body slumped over as he burst out laughing. When his head resurfaced, tears were rolling down his cheeks. He managed to stutter, "Oh, I wish I could have been there to see it. Oh, Lizzy, I'm so sorry. Tell me, I've got to know. What happened?"

She would have preferred not to tell him, but she knew he would just keep on bugging her about it forever until she did, so, reluctantly she told him what had happened in France up until the moment she switched on her own hall light. She had to pause at that specific moment, because Chris was buckling over with laughter again. Lizzy merely concentrated on the traffic and waited patiently.

By the time they reached the school Chris was calming down, shaking his head and wiping away the last of his tears.

"God, Lizzy, you never cease to amaze me. I mean, I knew you wouldn't mind me letting them stay at your place while you were gone, but that you let them stay on! So I take it you're all getting along fine, then?"

Lizzy shrugged. "Yeah."

"So how come you're picking up the little one?"

While she kept an eye out for Emily, Lizzy explained how Judith had managed to get work in the homecare sector and that it was easier for Lizzy to pick Emily up from school on Wednesdays due to their schedules.

Less than half an hour later Emily was scrambling alongside other children on a jungle gym and Lizzy and Chris were seated on a bench nearby keeping an eye on her.

"So tell me, how are you doing, honestly?" Chris was no longer teasing her and a part of Lizzy wished he were so that she wouldn't have to answer his questions.

"Fine. We're just about ready to start shooting. Things are going unnaturally well. The whole crew is waiting for the other shoe to drop."

"That's great, Lizzy, but I meant how are *you* doing?"

They'd been friends long enough to know when the other was deflecting and cared enough about each other to try and prick through the barrier, but Lizzy wasn't in the mood for sharing her feelings. She hadn't been in a long time.

"Like I said, fine. How about you and Tom? Frightened any crocodiles while you were over there?"

"Jeez, Liz, you're going to have to come up with another answer to that question. It would make it all that more believable."

"What? You asked me how I was and I told you fine. It's not my fault you don't believe me."

Chris shook his head, but let the matter go. "Have you got plans for Friday night?"

"No, why?"

"Well my neighbor mentioned that a new gay bar had opened while I was away and I was thinking of getting a group together to go check it out. What do you say?"

"I don't think so, Chris."

"Oh, come on, Lizzy. It is time for you to start having some fun again."

His words angered her and it cost her an enormous amount of strength not to lash out.

Chris gently placed a hand on her arm. "I'm sorry, Liz. I didn't mean it like that. We miss you, that's all."

Lizzy missed them too. She missed her old life, period, but without Maurice it would never be the same. How could she go out with her old friends and see them together with their partners while all she had was the vast void she carried inside her? She understood that to them three years might seem long enough for her to be able to move on, but how do you move on when a part of your soul is missing? Chris nudged her. "Apparently they've even got a pool table." He wriggled his eyebrows.

Lizzy knew he meant well and that he worried about her. Maybe if she went just this one time it would prove to him that he needn't worry. "Oh well, in that case."

"Excellent! Why don't you bring Judith?"

"Yeah, right."

"Why not? I thought you said things were good between you two?"

"They are."

"Well then?"

Lizzy picked up a pebble and threw it. "I haven't told her I'm gay."

Chris raised his hands in the air, exasperated. "So?"

"So, I don't want her to know."

Chris's mouth fell open in surprise.

Lizzy frowned. "If I were you, I'd shut that before you catch a fly in it."

"Since when has it been important to you to keep that a secret?"

"I'm not keeping it a secret. It's just I don't want her feeling even more awkward around me than she already does. I want to keep things simple."

"I don't think Judith's homophobic, if that's what you're implying, Liz."

"That's not what I'm saying. My sexuality is nobody's business but my own, but you know yourself, even people who are okay with it can still act differently in certain situations. Her awkwardness would make me feel uneasy and I really don't need that, especially not in the home I built with Maurice."

"Well, promise me you'll think about it."

Lizzy agreed, simply because it was Chris who was asking. "All right, I'll think about it. So, what do you say to an ice cream?"

❖

After dinner Lizzy retired to her study to do some work, but found herself thinking about Chris's invitation to check out the new bar. Since she'd lost Maurice, the idea of socializing with other people for fun had been the furthest from her mind. It still was, and she was surprised that she was even contemplating it. She heard Judith pass by her door and got up and followed her to the kitchen.

"Chris called today. He's back on home turf again."

"I was wondering when he'd turn up. I knew he'd be back sometime this week. I bet he was surprised to find out we're still here."

Lizzy had a flashback of Chris doubled over in laughter. "A little."

"Did he have a good time?"

"Yep, and I'm sure he'll tell you all about it the first chance he gets. He wants to get a group of people together to try out this new bar he's heard about. He wondered if we wanted to go."

"Sounds like fun. Are you going?"

"I don't know."

"When is it?"

"Friday."

Judith frowned and averted her eyes. "I can't Friday. I'm meeting someone."

During the time that Judith had been living in her home, Lizzy had never known her go out on an evening. The fact that she was planning to on Friday surprised her and she felt strangely curious. The word *who* was on the tip of her tongue, but she told herself it wasn't really any of her business.

"Okay. Well I'll let Chris know in the morning." Lizzy started to walk away, but Judith spoke quickly.

"I've arranged to meet Menno on Friday."

Lizzy turned back to face her, this time unable to hide her surprise. "Is that a good idea?"

"I have to see him sooner or later. There are things that need to be sorted out. I want to make sure that he keeps to his obligations regarding Emily, and seeing as she's got her sleepover party on Friday, I thought it was the best time."

It was clear to Lizzy that Judith was just as unhappy about the idea as she was, but she also realized that it needed to happen. She still didn't like the idea of Judith being alone with this Menno though.

"Where are you meeting him?"

"At a restaurant. I wanted to meet on neutral ground, and he insisted on having dinner." Judith sighed. "It was a compromise."

"Will you be all right?"

Judith smiled faintly. "I think so. It has to happen sooner or later, and I'd rather get it over and done with."

Lizzy didn't know what else to say. A part of her wanted to

convince Judith not to go. She didn't want Judith to be hurt any more than she had been, but she knew there was little she could do about it.

Chapter Twelve

Judith studied the woman in her mirror and questioned her motives.

Lizzy had offered to drop Emily off at her sleepover, and as soon as they had left Judith had started getting ready for her meeting with Menno. She'd showered, shaved her legs, plucked her eyebrows, and done her nails. She'd also ironed the cocktail dress she was going to wear, a simple but elegant black dress, with a side cut reaching up to her right upper thigh. When she'd first unpacked just over a month ago, she had been annoyed to find that she had unknowingly brought it with her. At the time she couldn't imagine ever needing it again and had left it crumpled in her suitcase. Yesterday, though, as she had riffled through her clothes wondering what she should wear, she found it again and decided she wanted to look stunning.

The idea of arriving at the restaurant looking her best had somehow felt empowering, but now, as she stood in front of the mirror applying the last of her makeup, doubt started to creep in and she questioned her motives. Was she really dressing up for herself or was she falling back into the old habit of trying to look her best for him? She stared at the woman in front of her and felt she didn't know her as well as she should. Who was she and what did she want? She'd already spent most of the night awake pondering over her decision to leave Menno. This would be the first time she would have to confront him and, more importantly, not lose her resolve.

She knew that after tonight, there would be no going back. Did she really have the courage and was she strong enough to go through life alone?

In the distance she heard the front door closing, indicating Lizzy had returned, and a few seconds later Lizzy called out to her.

"Judith, your taxi's arrived."

Hearing Lizzy's voice somehow made her feel a little more confident. Looking in the mirror one more time, she took a deep breath and then headed down the hall. Lizzy was kindly holding out her coat for her and Judith noticed how Lizzy's eyes quickly roamed over her. She felt an urgent need to explain something to Lizzy, but didn't know what or how.

"You…" Lizzy hesitated. "Look lovely."

Judith felt her cheeks flare up and was grateful she had an excuse to look the other way as she slipped her arms into the sleeves of her coat.

"I just wanted to look good, you know? Let him see what he's going to miss or something like that."

"If he doesn't know that already, then he never deserved you in the first place."

Judith's cheeks flared even more and she pretended to fully concentrate on the buttons of her coat.

"I don't know how long I'll be, but I don't expect to be gone long. What I have to say to Menno is simple enough."

Lizzy opened the door for her. "I'll be here if you need me."

Judith looked up at her and found gentle, concerned eyes looking back at her. She managed a thank-you before stepping out onto the landing.

❖

Before entering the restaurant Judith took a moment to gather her composure and muster up the strength she knew she would need to get through this. A part of her wanted to turn around and go back;

the other part desperately wanted to do this. Throughout the past few days all she had done was think about tonight, but during the taxi ride there all she had been able to think about was the way Lizzy had looked at her and the way her compliment had made her feel. Hearing that Lizzy thought she looked lovely pleased her in a way no other comment ever had. She couldn't quite explain it and guessed it had something to do with the fact that it had been a very long time since someone had complimented her about her looks.

The headwaiter took her coat and informed her that her dinner partner was already seated. A younger man stepped forward and led Judith to her table. She had never been to this particular restaurant before, but it was clear by its décor, the intimate setting, and the manner in which she was being treated that this was an expensive restaurant.

Menno stood when he noticed them approaching and his expression was one of smug satisfaction.

"You look wonderful, Judith."

He went to kiss her, but Judith turned her head so that his kiss landed on her cheek. He paused briefly before stepping in front of the headwaiter and pulled out her chair for her. It had been a long time since he had treated her so gentlemanly, but she knew it was a façade. Menno knew how to be a gentleman. It just wasn't his first nature to be one.

"I took the liberty of ordering for us both. Boeuf Stroganoff, your favorite."

Judith had never liked it when he had ordered for the both of them, but she had always told herself it was a form of togetherness and had accepted it without scorn. Now it irritated her that he thought he knew what she wanted. She felt compelled to say something sarcastic, like she fancied chicken, but she bit down on her words and politely replied, "Thank you, Menno."

A silence fell between them, a silence that for the moment suited Judith as she tried to acclimate herself to her surroundings. Menno, on the other hand, seemed uncomfortable with it.

"I'm glad you finally called. I didn't know where you were. I've been really worried. I must have called you on your cell a thousand times."

Judith had expressly kept her cell phone switched off since leaving him, anticipating his calls. She'd feared speaking to him, scared that she wouldn't be able to stand her ground. It had taken her this long to dig up the courage to face him and she wondered just how worried he'd been. If he had truly wanted to find them, then all he had had to do was to go to Emily's school. Menno continued his act of victim.

"You left without a word, only a note." He paused. "I've missed you."

It had been a long time since Menno had said anything remotely affectionate to her. For that same length of time she had hoped for a mere glimmer of affection from him, but now that he had showed it, she was surprised to find that his remark evoked no feeling whatsoever. A few weeks ago it would have been all he had needed to say to keep her from leaving him.

Her ongoing silence seemed to frustrate him.

"Aren't you going to say anything?"

Judith took a deep breath, ready to say what she had come to say. "I haven't come here to patch things up, Menno. I've come in the hope of finding a common ground concerning Emily."

His smile faded away and his eyes turned cold.

"Common ground?"

Judith took another deep breath and concentrated on keeping her nerve. "Yes, common ground. We need to be mature about our new situation. Not necessarily for ourselves, but for Emily's sake."

"Do you take me for a fool?"

Judith expressly withheld from answering the question.

"So this dinner is just about practicalities?"

"Our daughter is anything but a practicality."

Menno snorted and Judith did her best to stay calm.

"This dinner is about two parents taking responsibility for their child."

"Ah, come off it. We both know what this is about. There's another man in your life, isn't there? And don't even try to deny it." He leaned forward and gritted his teeth. "How else would you explain this new attitude of yours?"

Judith had heard this many times before. The accusation had always hurt her and she had always done her best to convince him otherwise. Now, instead of feeling hurt, she felt angry. Not just angry at him for believing her capable of adultery, but angry at herself for having always accepted his accusations and thus devaluing herself.

The thumping of her heart pounded in her ears, but she concentrated on keeping her voice as level as she could and looked Menno straight in the eye. "This attitude, as you so delicately put it, is that of a free woman taking back control of her life."

"If you think I'm going to support you as a free woman in this so-called new life of yours, think again. Let your new loverboy do that. Or is he the type that leads simple women to his bed, but not his bank?"

She wanted to scream at him, hit him, pull at his hair, anything to make him see. "All I ever wanted was to love you and have you love me back. It was all Emily ever wanted from you as well, but through your egotism and your closeted inferiority complex you were too blind to see how devoted we were to you."

Menno opened his mouth to speak, but Judith continued.

"That time has come and gone. You and I no longer have any obligations toward each other. I have nothing more to give you and I no longer want anything from you. Emily, on the other hand, whether you like it or not, accept it or not, is your daughter, and you will fulfill your obligations to her."

Menno was right in her face. "How dare you speak to me like this? Why don't you talk to your new lover about obligations? For all we know, he may be her real father."

Judith stood, knowing she had to go while she still could. "If you can't be mature about this, you leave me no other choice but to do this the hard way. You'll be hearing from a lawyer shortly. Goodbye, Menno."

He rose abruptly to his feet. "Who the hell do you think you are?"

She forced herself to look him straight in the eye one last time. "Whatever the answer may be to that question, it no longer concerns you."

With that said, she turned and walked away from him, coaxing her trembling legs to work with her, pleading that they held out, at least until she was outside.

As she walked down the street in the freezing cold she realized two things. One, she had forgotten her coat, and second, her relationship with Menno was finished. There was no going back. She had closed a chapter in her life, permanently. She had no idea what lay ahead of her or what the next chapter would entail, but whatever it was, she had just entered it.

❖

When Judith opened the front door, the numbness that had engulfed her on the long walk home gave way to an overwhelming feeling of sadness. As she closed the door behind her she started to cry. She struggled not to, but she had no strength left and her body started to shake uncontrollably.

"Judith?"

Judith felt an arm around her shoulders.

"God, you're freezing!"

Judith tried to speak, but she couldn't.

Lizzy's voice was gentle in her ear. "Come on."

Judith tried to walk, but her legs would no longer cooperate and she staggered. Lizzy caught her in time and Judith felt herself being lifted off the ground. Before she knew it she was on the couch with a blanket wrapped around her. She thought she heard Lizzy say something about a bath, but her own sobbing drowned out the words. She fought to try to control her body and the flood of tears, but she was defenseless against the onslaught of raw emotion.

An eternity passed and all that there was were her tears and the flood of emotions freeing themselves after years of captivity. Gradually, her body's shaking calmed to mere trembling and the flooding tears gave way to a light but consistent flow. She started to become aware of her surroundings again and realized she was cuddled up to Lizzy. She felt too exhausted to feel embarrassed, and the warmth of Lizzy's closeness was too comforting for her to care. She tried to speak, but her throat was too swollen.

"There's a hot bath waiting for you. It will do you good. It will get the chill out of your bones."

Judith didn't know what to think or say, but Lizzy slipped out from under her and stood, pulling her up with her. She felt dizzy and her head pounded, but she let Lizzy help her to the bathroom. Lizzy's kindness filled the empty holes left by the escaping emotions and Judith felt herself start to lose it again.

"I'm so sorry."

Lizzy pulled down the toilet lid and gestured for Judith to sit.

"I suggest you stay in the bath for as long as you can, and keep the water hot. It will minimize the severe cold you're going to get." Lizzy hesitated. "Will you be all right on your own?"

Judith managed a nod and Lizzy hesitated a moment longer before walking out of the bathroom.

Judith carefully stood and wriggled out of her dress, letting it fall unceremoniously to the floor. She freed herself from her underwear and with considerable concentration stepped into the bath. The water burned her skin and a pulse of heat coursed through her body, making the rest of her feel even colder than it already was. As she submerged herself, the stinging heat of the water transformed into a welcoming antidote, numbing the wretched feeling inside her. As she lay there, a calmness, like a warm blanket, wrapped itself around her heart and bones, bringing with it an overwhelming feeling of tiredness. The events of the evening seemed far off, like a scene from a movie watched long ago.

Memories from the past appeared before her, then disappeared, making way for others: the curtains closing behind her father's casket just before its contents were consumed by flames; the first time Menno had accused her of having an affair; the first time she had held Emily in her arms, and the card she had received from her sister shortly thereafter. She saw her mother all dressed up, commanding instructions to caterers, complaining about their lack of enthusiasm. She saw Mrs. Eijk waving her hands about in an enthusiastic gesture, she saw herself walking down the school corridor toward her first class as a teacher. She slid farther into the bath and dunked her head under the hot water. A jolt of sensation shot down her spine. She stayed like that for a while as more images appeared, faster and faster until they were just a blur. When her veins screamed beneath her skin she pulled herself up, taking in deep breaths. She felt naked, not just physically but emotionally, and she felt extremely raw, but with these feelings came an immense sense of purity.

She pulled at the plug chain and stepped out of the bath. For a moment the room blurred and her legs went weak. She grabbed hold of the side of the bath, focusing on her grip until the dizziness subsided. Her whole body felt heavy, making the task of drying herself off slow and tedious. The dressing gown Lizzy never wore was hanging on a hook on the back of the door and she felt compelled to put it on. That night when Lizzy had arrived unexpectedly, she had put it on in her panic, not giving it a second thought. Now as she wrapped herself up in the dressing gown, she was fully aware of what she was doing. For some reason the idea of wearing something of Lizzy's at that moment made her feel less raw and more safe. She left the bathroom just as the bath made its final orchestral sucking sound.

❖

The milk Lizzy was stirring had just started to rise when she heard the gurgling of the bath. She poured the hot milk into a mug, then added a big tablespoon of cocoa and stirred again.

For the past few years she had gone through life numb. It had been the only way she could cope, but during the past few weeks that numbness had started failing her, and tonight had been pivotal.

Throughout the evening she had tried several things to occupy her mind, but her thoughts had kept drifting back to Judith and her dinner with her ex. She'd been worried that Menno might convince Judith to go back with him, then she'd chastised herself for not trusting Judith's strength and capability in handling her own life. It was just that she knew all too well how bravery could disappear in an eyewink when entering a room of emotional confrontation, and she didn't want Judith or Emily to get hurt any more than they already had been. The fact that she considered Judith going back to Menno a mistake had made her feel even more annoyed at herself. At the end of the day, who was she to say they shouldn't give it another go if that's what they chose, but when she saw the state of Judith when she arrived back home she'd felt instant rage toward Menno, and the remnants of that anger still echoed inside her.

She had acted on autopilot, doing what she thought needed to be done without hesitation. She'd held Judith close in an attempt to help get her warm again while waiting for the bath to fill, but holding someone so close had made her sweat with fear. Memories of holding Maurice during her illness, trying in vain to soothe the pain, came flooding to the surface, and it had cost her all her strength to focus on helping Judith.

The door to Judith's bedroom was ajar and Lizzy could see Judith sitting on her bed gazing out in front of her. She looked exhausted and drawn, and reminded her yet again of Maurice when her illness had first started to take its toll, when she could no longer hide her pain and the exhaustion in coping with it. Lizzy shook her head, trying to shake the memory and the emotions that came with it. She entered the room, but was careful to avoid eye contact.

"I've made you a hot drink that will help you sleep." Lizzy handed Judith the mug before stepping back to the doorway again. "I've also put a hot water bottle in your bed."

"Is that a gift you were born with or is it something you've learned through the years?"

"What?"

"Knowing what to say and do at the right time?"

Lizzy thought back to all the times she had wanted to say something to Maurice, something that would make a difference, and all the times she had failed. She struggled to cope with the heavy churning in her chest.

"You should get yourself into bed."

Judith managed a weak smile and did exactly that.

❖

Lizzy felt mentally drained as she undressed for bed, but the last bit of her working brain made her set the alarm clock before crawling under the sheets, because she doubted that Judith would be well enough to pick Emily up in the morning. Then, like she always did, she rolled over and stared at the empty space Maurice still filled, desperately trying to recapture her warm expression. Normally she would fall asleep while doing so, but tonight she couldn't hold on to her. It was if she was slowly losing the ability to remember what she had looked like, and the thought filled her with self-loathing. She closed her eyes and remembered how Judith had looked when she had arrived home. Shaking, cold, hurt by the man who proclaimed to love her.

People understood that they would one day die, and yet they still walked through life oblivious to how precious their time was. So many used that time chasing after things that eventually meant nothing and did so while hurting those around them. Deep in her heart she knew the value of someone's life couldn't be measured with conceptions of good or bad, but she would never understand how certain people got to live out their lives with such disregard while others got hurt and people like her Maurice, a warm kind soul, had to die so young and so cruelly.

CHAPTER THIRTEEN

Lizzy opened her eyes to see the red digits on her alarm clock pointedly glaring back at her. It was twenty to nine. She'd woken ten minutes before the alarm was set to go off. For some reason that made her feel smug, as if she'd somehow won one over on it. She rolled onto her back and considered closing her eyes again, but she didn't know whether Judith was up yet and if she was even well enough to pick Emily up. She forced herself up and away from the warmth of her bed and trudged down the hall imagining the alarm clock secretly gloating at her behind her back. She listened at Judith's door for any indication that she was up, but the whole apartment echoed silence. She politely knocked and waited for a sound. When none came, she carefully opened the door. Judith was dead to the world and Lizzy couldn't bring herself to wake her up. She quietly closed the door and headed for the bathroom.

Lizzy rang the doorbell and waited until a well-dressed woman answered. Despite her clothing she looked worn out and Lizzy sympathized with her. She imagined it was no easy task hosting a sleepover for a bunch of seven-year-olds.

"Hi, I'm here to pick up Emily."

The woman seemed to hesitate before offering her hand. "I'm sorry, but I don't believe we've met before."

"No. I believe it was your husband whom I spoke to yesterday when I dropped Emily off. I'm Lizzy, a..." She hesitated, trying to find the words that best described her relationship to Judith. "Friend of Judith's."

The woman still seemed hesitant and Lizzy understood her predicament. She wouldn't feel comfortable handing over a child to someone she had never met before, especially if she hadn't been told to. She felt she needed to elaborate to help put the woman at ease.

"Judith's come down with a bad cold and asked me to pick Emily up for her."

"Oh, I hope it's not too serious."

"It will probably pass in a few days."

Just then, the man Lizzy had spoken to the day before stepped into the hallway carrying a child in his arms. The woman turned and called to him. "Henk, you remember Lizzy from yesterday?"

The man waved with his free hand and the woman seemed to accept this as a confirmation that all was well. She turned to Lizzy with a warm smile.

"Well, I'll just go fetch her, then."

Lizzy waited on the doorstep until Emily ran into the hall enthusiastically calling out her name.

"Lizzy! Look what I've got!"

Emily ran up to her, her coat dragging in one hand and a bag of sweets dangling from the other.

"Wow!" Lizzy took the bag, pretending to admire it.

"We all got one. Everybody else ate most of theirs last night, but I've been saving mine."

The woman seemed to completely relax at witnessing Emily's enthusiasm at seeing Lizzy and passed her Emily's small backpack.

"She's such a lovely child. So easily pleased."

"Yes, she is." Lizzy knelt to help Emily put on her coat and zip up.

"Give Judith my best wishes, won't you."

"I will, and thank you for having Emily over. She seems to have really enjoyed herself."

"It was a pleasure. Like I said, she's a lovely girl."

Lizzy shook the woman's hand one more time and then led Emily down the path to the car.

"How come Mommy's not here?"

"She's not feeling very well, but she'll be all right. She's wrapped up nice and warm in bed and with a lot of TLC she'll be just fine."

"TLC?"

"Yes, TLC. It means tender loving care."

Emily wrinkled her eyebrows together. "You mean lots of hugs and kisses?"

Lizzy smiled. "Yep."

Emily repeated the letters to herself as she climbed into the backseat.

When they got back Emily said that she was going to give her mommy lots of TLC and ran straight to Judith's room, but came back out tiptoeing and whispered that mommy was still asleep. Lizzy made them both a drink and listened patiently as Emily recounted every minute detail about the sleepover. By the end of it Lizzy knew the names of all the girls there and their take on the boys at school, plus the names of the latest preteen idols and the gossip that surrounded them. She couldn't remember her elementary school days being so complex. She gathered this was what the experts meant when they said that the youth of today was much older than the youth of prior generations, or was this a case of the older you get, the more you forget?

After Emily finished telling her story, Lizzy asked about her homework and they sat together at the dinner table while Emily attempted to solve her row of sums. To Lizzy's relief, the math homework of a seven-year-old wasn't all that difficult and she was easily able to help her.

❖

Judith slowly opened her eyes and listened to her own breathing. The events of the previous night came flooding back and she buried her face in her pillow, trying to hide from the ugly feelings that accompanied them. Then she remembered Emily and lifted her head to look at the time. It was five o'clock p.m. Stunned, she stared at the numbers with disbelief. There was no way she could have slept so long. She quickly stood, but the room started to sway and she was forced to sit back down on the bed and wait for the dizziness to subside. Her second attempt at getting up proved successful, although she still felt unsteady as she crossed the room.

As soon as she opened her bedroom door she was hit by the familiar smell of pancakes and recognized the cheerful bantering of Emily in the distance. Relief swept through her knowing Emily was safely back at home.

"What if I drop it?"

"Then we'll just make another one."

Emily giggled nervously.

"I tell you what, I'll count to three and then you just flick it like I showed you. Okay? Ready? One…two…three…"

Judith watched from the doorway as Emily closed her eyes, stretched out her arms, and then tossed the pancake. It just about made enough height to flip itself over, but landed half in and half out of the pan.

"See, there's nothing to it," Lizzy said.

"But it's hanging over the side." Emily pouted.

"That's all right, just give the pan a slight shake until it…there you go. See, it just slides back in."

"Hey, I did it!" Emily was grinning again.

"You sure did."

Deep down Judith knew Lizzy would have taken care of things and she was eternally grateful to her for looking after Emily, but seeing them together in the kitchen making pancakes, seeing how much Emily was enjoying herself also made her feel a little redundant.

She cleared her throat and joined them.

"Mommy, I just helped Lizzy make pancakes and I flipped one as well."

Judith perched herself on a bar stool on the other side of the counter and avoided looking at Lizzy, not wanting her to see her watery eyes.

"Yes, darling, I saw you."

"You did?"

"Yes, dear, and you were great." Judith smiled lovingly at her.

"Shall I show you again?"

She wanted to be here, sharing these moments with Emily, but she felt so tired. Her whole body ached and she could feel a migraine coming on. She tried to sound encouraging.

"I'd love that."

Emily, guided by Lizzy's hand, attempted to flip another pancake. This time the pancake landed perfectly back in the pan and Emily's expression was one of immense pride. Judith managed to clap enthusiastically, but then Emily offered to show her again. Judith wanted to indulge her, but her migraine was getting stronger and she was starting to feel nauseated.

Lizzy intervened. "Hey, Emily, how about we let your mommy go back to bed for a while so you can practice and then you can make her a pancake from scratch another time."

Emily turned to face Judith. "Are you still tired, Mommy?"

Emily's concerned expression made Judith want to cry again.

"Yes, darling, I am, but it's nothing for you to worry about."

Emily's expression turned resolute. "Then Lizzy is right, you should go back to bed."

Judith glanced at Lizzy for the first time, but she was looking at the floor. With a sigh, Judith stepped off the stool and reached across the counter to touch Emily's face. "I'm very lucky to have you as my daughter."

Emily grinned from ear to ear.

❖

Again Judith woke to the sound of her own breathing. This time, though, the room was pitch-black and there was silence all around. The numbers on the clock now flashed two a.m. She fumbled to locate the switch for the bedside lamp. After letting her eyes adjust to the light, she forced her body out of bed for a second time that day.

The hall was dark except for the glow from Emily's bedside light. She headed toward it and when she found Emily fast asleep, tucked in bed, safe and cozy, her mind swamped with emotion again. She hated the fact that she hadn't been there to tuck Emily into bed and felt upset with Lizzy for being the one to do it, and at the same time guilty with undefined gratitude that she had.

CHAPTER FOURTEEN

Lizzy got up and found a cheerful Emily in her usual post, in front of the TV watching her morning cartoons. Taking care of her yesterday hadn't been difficult, but the idea of being responsible for a child had been unnerving. Looking after her the whole day was very different from a few hours in the park. To Lizzy's dismay, Judith was nowhere to be seen and Lizzy guessed she was still asleep. When Judith had joined them in the kitchen yesterday looking so pale and drawn, she had reminded her of Maurice in those first days of her illness. Her insides had coiled and she'd only been able to cope by focusing all her attention on Emily. She had hoped that Judith would be feeling better today.

She made Emily breakfast and decided to boil an egg for Judith. She carried the breakfast tray to Judith's room, but found her still fast asleep. She placed the tray on the nightstand next to Judith's bed and stared at the form beneath the sheets, mesmerized by the soft sound of breathing and the slight rise of the body with each breath. She realized she was waiting for it to stop, for the silence to come, the sound of breathing to cease. She longed to hold Maurice again and feel her body wrapped in her arms, warm, safe, and alive.

She barely made it to the toilet in time. The hole in her chest churned ferociously, pain and anger escaping her depths. She gagged as wave after wave of emotions rose to the surface. Then she fell to the floor void of all sensation except for the realization that she was still alive.

An hour later she was at the studio staring into her coffee, willing her mind to crack into focus. There were only two weeks left before primary shooting started and she couldn't allow herself to fall apart now. Anita had scheduled this meeting and she needed to be clear-headed.

"Since when have we started hiring underage help?"

Lizzy didn't need to look up to know Anita was the one standing across the table from her.

"Aren't you the one who's always on about finding cheap labor?"

"Oh, that's sweet, even for you."

Anita sat opposite her and poured herself a fresh cup of coffee. Lizzy knew that Anita had been working her butt off getting things together before shooting started, and the bags under her eyes proved it.

"You look worn out."

"You don't look your best either, and your nightmare's yet to start."

Anita added four sugars to her coffee. "So, would you care to explain to me why a seven-year-old is playing with the gaffer?"

"She's the daughter of a friend."

"Would this friend happen be the woman who's living with you at the moment?"

Lizzy was surprised that Anita knew about that. Anita raised her hands in a gesture of innocence.

"I'm the producer, remember? It's my business to know everything, and besides, Sam and I had dinner the other night."

Lizzy had not intended on telling Sam about her new cohabitants, but after she'd had to cut one of her visits short for a second time to pick up Emily, he had become suspicious and had blackmailed her into telling him: *"Either you tell me what's going on and I'll show you the new changes to the storyboard, or you don't and I won't."*

Lizzy scowled. "And you guys had nothing better to do than talk about my life?"

Anita shrugged. "Normally yes, normally we skip all foreplay."

The image of Sam's spindly legs running up the stairs flashed into view and Lizzy winced. "Please, spare me the details."

"So how come the girl isn't at home with her mother?"

"Her mother's not feeling well, so I brought her along."

"I must admit I never expected to see you bringing a child to work."

"Yeah, well…" To Lizzy's dismay she realized she didn't have anything to say to that.

"Ah, don't look so uncomfortable, your secret's safe with me."

Lizzy frowned. "What secret?"

Anita smiled. "That you like kids."

Lizzy opened her mouth to respond, but just then a group of fellow crew members walked into the cafeteria area. Before they reached them, Anita leaned closer and whispered, "Maurice would be proud of you."

Anita's words floated before her for only a split second. After she'd thrown up her insides only a few hours ago, her usual numbness had given way to a vast emptiness and she was defenseless against Anita's words. They sank past her worn-out defenses and for a brief moment Lizzy considered the possibility that they might be true. The sound of scraping chairs filled the space around her and Emily appeared at her side with that million-dollar smile.

❖

From deep within her consciousness Judith registered the knock at her door.

"I'm sorry to wake you, but it's time for Emily's bath and I was wondering if you were well enough to take care of it. I mean I'd do it, but I don't want her feeling awkward or anything like that."

Without thinking Judith flipped back the sheets and forced

herself in an upright position. "No, no I'll do it." She rubbed her eyes. "What time is it?"

"It's nearly seven. Are you okay?"

"Yes, I'm fine." Judith spoke more sharply than she intended, but Lizzy had already disappeared before she could apologize.

She lingered on the edge of her bed, feeling like she was balancing herself on a seesaw—too much to one side and she would topple. She couldn't believe how terrible she felt. She didn't know if it was because of her nearly freezing to death or if it was due to the release of all that stopped-up emotion that had torn itself out of her the other day. Whatever the reason, she had never felt so exhausted, and the fact that she had slept nearly all weekend and had only seen Emily once upset her.

Earlier in the day she had awoken to find the apartment empty, and not knowing where Emily was had been like a thunderstrike to her heart. Then when she'd found the note left on the kitchen counter by Lizzy explaining where they were, her panic had turned to anger. Lizzy had taken Emily without consulting her first. She had wanted to be up for when they got back, but her new emotions had zapped the little strength she had and she had been forced to go back to bed again. Now she wanted nothing more than to see Emily.

While she helped Emily bathe, she listened as Emily told her about her day. The frustration within her gradually melted away as she listened and she secretly chastised herself for being a fool and for being selfish. Emily had been well looked after and had enjoyed herself immensely. Lizzy, who had let them stay in her home, who had been nothing but kind and supportive, had now taken care of Emily without hesitation. It was just that Emily was her life, and the idea of not being a good mother to her was unbearable. She wasn't used to not being one hundred percent available for Emily, and she certainly wasn't used to having someone around to help her out instead of making things more difficult. Lizzy taking care of Emily while she couldn't had been frightening, and she had unjustly projected her fear onto Lizzy in the form of anger.

What had made it worse was that she was very aware of

how happy and relaxed Emily seemed since they had arrived, and although Emily's laughter and cheerful banter warmed her soul, it tore at her heart, because it only reinforced that which she already knew to be true: Emily had not been happy in the life she had built for her. Emily seemed to have no trouble in accepting the changes in their lives and the absence of her father and, unlike Judith herself, seemed to have no trouble in accepting Lizzy's kindness.

Once Emily was settled for the night, Judith went to look for Lizzy. She found her drying up the dishes from the evening meal. She looked tired and Judith's guilt only grew.

"Emily asked me to say good night."

Lizzy glanced over her shoulder. "Thank you."

"I'm sorry about the way I was earlier."

"There's no need."

Lizzy was only a few feet away, but she sounded distant, and at that moment Judith wanted desperately to bridge the gap.

"Please, I need to apologize. What you've done for us, taking care of Emily last night and today, it's, it's…" Judith struggled to find the words. "I'm not used to not being there for her, and, well…"

Lizzy stopped what she was doing. "It's okay, Judith. I get it."

"Do you?"

"You're her mother. You're used to being the only one that takes care of her. She's your life. You love her and you're scared of losing her. I get it."

Judith felt the air in her lungs dissipate. The intensity with which Lizzy had spoken stunned her. Although those words were meant for her, she knew instinctively that in them lay the key to Lizzy's pain. She felt like she was on the verge of finally understanding something important about her, but Lizzy was already walking past her. She felt an uncontrollable urge to stop her, to ask her what it was she wasn't understanding, but she had no idea how. She felt worn out and resigned herself to yet again watching Lizzy walk away from her.

She checked in on Emily one last time before readily climbing back into bed.

❖

"Mommy, why aren't you getting up? The clock has been buzzing for ages."

Judith looked up at Emily and remembered it was Monday morning. She didn't need to look at the clock to know she was late.

"I'm sorry, darling." Judith sneezed. "Why don't you go ahead and get dressed. I'll be right behind you."

Emily didn't move. "I think you should stay in bed, Mommy. Like I have to when I'm sick."

Judith smiled and stroked Emily's hair. "I wouldn't call lying on the couch watching cartoons all day the same as staying in bed."

Emily chuckled and Judith rested her heavy head back on her pillow. She didn't feel well enough to go to work, but she told herself it was simply a case of mind over matter.

"Go on, now, and don't forget to brush your teeth."

Emily still didn't move and her expression turned stern. "I really don't think you should get up, Mommy."

Judith couldn't help it; the tears came of their own accord. Emily started gently shaking her arm, asking her what was the matter, but Judith couldn't answer her and buried her face into the pillow as Emily ran out of the room.

Lizzy, like the previous nights, had only managed a few hours' sleep, but she was quickly awake when she realized that Emily was next to her bed trying to wake her up.

"What's the matter, Emily?"

"It's Mommy. She's crying."

Emily was clearly distressed, so Lizzy let herself be led by the hand to Judith's room, where she found Judith lying in bed crying into her pillow. Lizzy didn't think she could handle this, but the look on Emily's face made her stay. She asked her if she could have a moment alone with her mother and waited until Emily was out of the room before kneeling next to the bed. She gently placed a hand on Judith's shoulder. "Judith?"

"Leave…me…alone, please." Judith could hardly get the words out.

Lizzy spoke softly. "Judith, would you look at me, please?"

"I can't."

"Why not?"

"Because I can't stop crying."

"That's nothing to be ashamed of."

Judith mumbled into the pillow and Lizzy had to lean in closer to understand what she was saying.

"My seven-year-old daughter thinks her mother should stay in bed. I can't believe how things have turned out and I can't believe what a wreck I am. I thought leaving Menno was what I wanted, but what I wanted was a family. I wanted someone to love and love me back. I wanted Emily to be loved and safe. She doesn't even miss her own father. What does that tell you and what does it say about me as a mother? My father once said that all he expected of me was for me to be myself, but I've failed him and I've failed Emily and on top of all that I'm feeling utterly sorry for myself and I've got a horrible cold."

Judith lost herself in sobs again and Lizzy wondered what on earth she could say to make things better. They hadn't spoken about what had happened that night between Judith and Menno, but Lizzy understood that the confrontation had triggered these emotions. Although Judith had seemed to be coping well up until then, Lizzy appreciated the fact that Judith had a lot to confront within herself before she was ready to move on, and she knew all too well what it felt like to fail someone you loved. Without thinking she started to stroke Judith's hair.

"I've never met your father, but from what you've told me about him I don't think he would see you as a failure. If anything, I think he would be proud of you for being brave enough to try to change your life, and as for Emily, that little girl knows what it is to be loved. She knows how much you love her. You haven't failed, Judith, not by a long shot."

"I'm not usually like this, Lizzy."

"I know."

"I feel like a silly little girl."

"You're hurt. You have been for a long time. You've just found out about it and now your body is trying to heal itself."

Her own words rang too true in her own ears and with a sigh she stopped playing with the soft strands of hair between her fingers.

"How about I call your work and let them know that you're sick."

"I can't."

"Of course you can. You just have to stay put while you learn to accept that things have changed and that you don't have to feel guilty about it. I'll see to Emily."

Judith turned to her. "You are the kindest person I have ever known."

Lizzy started to rise, but Judith reached out and grabbed her arm. "Please, Lizzy, accept my compliment."

Lizzy hesitated, not quite sure how to. "You're an easy person to be kind to."

Judith smiled softly. "That feels like only half an acceptance, but it will do for now."

Lizzy smiled back and started to rise again. "I'll see to Emily."

"No, wait. I don't want her going to school with the image of me sobbing in her head. I want to try to make her breakfast, or at least see her off."

Lizzy reached for her dressing gown that lay at the end of Judith's bed and passed it to her. "That sounds like a good idea to me."

CHAPTER FIFTEEN

By Wednesday Judith was starting to feel much better again. She had slept through most of the past few days, leaving Emily primarily in Lizzy's care, but she had made a point of being there to tuck her in at night. Today, when she'd awoken around midday, she had felt the need to do something constructive and had set about preparing dinner. Both Lizzy and Emily had protested when they arrived home to find her in the kitchen, but their protests had ended at the table when they had all sat to eat. She had just tucked Emily in to bed and was in the process of climbing back into her own when she heard a quiet knock on her bedroom door.

"Yes?"

The door opened and Lizzy popped her head in. "Can I speak to you for a moment?"

Judith gestured for her to come in. Lizzy entered and quietly pushed the door to and hovered at the end of Judith's bed.

"You know that Emily's got that audition on Monday…"

Judith raised an eyebrow. "You mean the audition she isn't allowed to do?"

Lizzy smiled. "Yeah, that one."

"Uh-huh."

"I was wondering if you'd allow me to get her a pirate costume, you know, to buff up her chances."

Judith didn't know what to say. There was a sparkle in Lizzy's eyes that she'd never seen before, and her whole manner was endearing.

"You know, I think that's a lovely idea."

"You do?"

"Absolutely. I just wish I could be there to see Mrs. Bouwman's face when Emily walks on stage dressed up as a pirate when she's supposed to be a fairy."

"I've never met Mrs. Bouwman, but I think I would enjoy that too." Lizzy hesitated a moment before continuing. "How about I pop back home tomorrow while she's still at school, and we go get one. That's if you're up to it, of course."

Lizzy's attempt at keeping her involved as well as her attentiveness touched her immensely.

"Have you got the time?"

Lizzy shrugged. "Well, we're in the final stages of setting everything up now, so I'm sure I can sneak away for an extended lunch break, and besides, I'm the director. I'm supposed to have some say in what goes on, on set." She wriggled her eyebrows. "I'll just have to make sure Anita doesn't catch me leaving. So, are we on?"

Lizzy's playful innocence was a striking contrast to her usual aloofness, and the fact that Lizzy obviously felt safe enough with her to show that side of herself did her heart good. There was no way she could have said no to her, even if she had wanted to.

"Yes, we're on. What time did you have in mind?"

"Is eleven okay?"

"Sounds good to me."

Lizzy turned serious. "If you don't feel well enough, call me. Don't force anything."

"I will."

"Promise?"

"Yes, I promise."

Lizzy seemed to relax again. "Okay. Well, I'll let you get to sleep."

She turned to leave, but Judith couldn't help herself. "Do you know the saying, whatever you give out you get double back?"

"Yes."

"You have a lot to expect."

Judith tried to keep eye contact in an attempt to make sure that Lizzy understood what she meant, but Lizzy averted her gaze.

"I've already had my share. Good night, Judith."

"Good night, Lizzy."

❖

The first thing Lizzy did when she arrived on set the following morning was to schedule an extra-long lunch break for herself. It hadn't been easy and Anita was pissed at first, but then offered Emily her moral support after Lizzy had explained about the situation with Mrs. Bouwman.

She felt excited and couldn't remember when she'd last felt excited about anything. She was sure she was being daft. After all it was only a kids' school play, but she really wanted Emily to have the right gear to give it her best shot. She was pleasantly surprised to find Judith already waiting for her on the pavement and was glad to see she had some color back in her cheeks.

"Hey, you didn't have to wait outside. I would have come up and gotten you."

Judith closed the car door and reached for her seat belt. "I know, but I've been stuck indoors for days now, and besides, I'm looking forward to this little excursion."

Lizzy started to pull away from the curb. "You look lovely, by the way."

After several days of bed and snotty tears, Judith wanted to look like a normal human being again and had made an extra effort in getting ready. It touched her immensely that Lizzy had noticed.

"You're just used to seeing me look a mess."

"You didn't look a mess the other night."

Judith knew she was referring to the night she'd gone to see Menno, and her cheeks flushed as they had when Lizzy had complimented her that night. She quickly turned away to look out of her window.

As soon as they entered the costume shop, they were distracted from their search by the extravagance of some of the costumes. They roamed the aisles, picking ones out as they went along, making each other laugh and giggling sheepishly together at some of the more naughty-looking ones. Eventually the shop assistant, whose somber face was a sharp contrast to the items on sale, approached them and asked them if they needed help. When they explained to her what they were looking for, she coldly informed them that they didn't sell costumes for children and barely managed the courtesy of telling them of another shop that did.

The next shop did sell children's costumes and they found the cutest pirate costume they had ever seen. In their excitement they decided to buy an extra-long sword and a long black wig to go with it. While they waited to check out, Lizzy's stomach growled. She checked the time and knew she should be heading back to the studio, but she was enjoying her time with Judith.

"Would you like to have lunch somewhere?"

Judith was clearly surprised at her suggestion. "Shouldn't you be getting back?"

"I still have time."

Judith smiled shyly. "Well, I am feeling a bit peckish."

Lizzy's mind was made up. "Well, that settles it, then." Lizzy took her to an Irish pub, the O'Reilly's next to the Royal Palace, and soon they were seated at a heavy wooden table overlooking the street with a crackling fireplace just a few feet away.

Judith took a sip of her coffee. "I can't remember when I last went out for lunch just for the fun of it, and this is such a romantic setting."

Lizzy enjoyed seeing the sparkle in Judith's eyes and was glad she had suggested coming here.

Time seemed to stand still as they chatted, and it wasn't until after their plates had been cleared away and they were drinking their second cup of coffee that Lizzy finally looked at her watch. She was late and although she would have preferred to stay and listen to Judith, she knew she couldn't.

"I have to get back," she said apologetically.

"Have I got time to pay the ladies' room a visit? I mean, I don't want to get you in even more trouble than you already are."

"Ah, Anita's bark is bigger than her bite."

"She sounds like an interesting character."

"She is." Lizzy casually reached out and took Judith's coat and held it up for her. "If you want, I could arrange it that you come with me next Saturday."

Judith slipped into her coat and then turned to face Lizzy with a beaming smile. "I'd love that."

❖

Judith kicked off her shoes and let herself fall back onto the couch. She felt tired, but she also felt a gentle buzz of excitement. The past few hours with Lizzy had been so cozy, and at no time had Lizzy put up a barrier or retreated into herself. Judith knew that was most likely due to the fact that they hadn't really talked about anything too personal. However, this had been the first time they had been able to be around each other for a lengthy period of time without things turning awkward, and Judith reveled in the notion.

Just before Lizzy had dropped her off back at home, Judith had told her that she needn't worry about picking up Emily from school that afternoon because she felt well enough to do it herself. They had also arranged to talk later that night, if Lizzy got back on time, about when to give Emily her present. She didn't need to be at the school for another few hours so she closed her eyes, sinking farther back into the cushions, and hoped Lizzy didn't have to work late.

❖

As was usual when Lizzy worked, she forgot about the outside world and the passage of time. The only thing that mattered to her in those moments was getting the designated scene right, and that process was independent of time constraints, no matter what Anita said.

Most of the crew had left hours ago, but a small group had stayed behind to finish going over the planned shots for the following day. So when they finally decided to wrap it up for the day, she was surprised to see how late it was. She knew that even if Judith had tried to stay up for her she would most likely already be in bed by the time she got back.

As she expected, the apartment was quiet and in near darkness when she arrived home. She had made it clear to Judith that she might not make it back on time, but she still felt a bit guilty and also a little disappointed. She'd been looking forward to planning Emily's present with her.

That night her recurring dream of falling down a shaft was replaced by a dream in which Maurice stood surrounded by children in some kind of orphanage. The other adults weren't aware of Maurice's presence. Only the children could see her. Maurice was walking among them, speaking softly to the children and making them smile. For the first time in three years Lizzy awoke and looked over at Maurice's side of the bed and dared wonder if maybe, just maybe, Maurice wasn't actually gone, but that she was still out there somewhere, somehow.

Chapter Sixteen

Judith had stayed up until eleven o'clock waiting for Lizzy to come home. Then she'd gone to bed with the hope of catching her early in the morning instead. When she awoke to find Lizzy already gone she had at first felt disappointed, but she had quickly pushed the feeling aside, telling herself that maybe Lizzy leaving so early was an indication that she might be able to get back earlier tonight.

After dropping Emily off at school she returned home and called the job center to let them know that she would be able to work again on Monday. Then she decided the apartment could do with a tidy up. So she riffled through Lizzy's CD collection, chose a compilation of fifties music, and set about dancing through the dust.

Menno had always been picky and controlling, making the chore of cleaning their home a stressful responsibility, but today Judith laughed while she worked. She laughed at him and at herself: *How the hell can someone make a mistake when vacuuming and what the hell does it matter anyway?*

So as the divas of the fifties accompanied her around the apartment, she stepped even farther away from her old life, and with every piece of clothing she picked up and with every sweep of the vacuum, she felt she was coming home to herself.

She felt tired afterward but wasn't ready to give in to her fatigue, so she set about preparing dinner. She understood that now that shooting had started she would see even less of Lizzy, but she secretly hoped Lizzy would make it back on time tonight. She knew it was unfair to hope for such a thing, but she felt happy and for some reason she wanted to share that with Lizzy just as much as she wanted to share Emily's gift with her.

❖

As soon as Lizzy opened the door she recognized the aroma of garlic and onions and realized she was ravenous. She was pleased to see that the light in the living room was on, indicating that Judith was still up. She had tried to make it home earlier than yesterday, but it was still after ten o'clock and she'd been worried that she might have missed Judith again. She quickly hung her jacket up and turned to see Judith standing at the end of the hallway.

"Are you hungry?"

"I am now." Lizzy spoke a little too enthusiastically and Judith's smile broadened.

"You don't know what I've made yet."

"True, but it smells absolutely divine."

"I'm sure I can scrape enough leftovers together, as long as you don't mind eating food that's been in the bin."

Lizzy wasn't sure how to respond. She wasn't used to Judith teasing her like this, but found the mischievous twinkle in her eyes enticing. She pretended to seriously consider the question.

"That depends. Was the bin clean when you threw it in or was it—"

"Let's stop right there, shall we?" Judith screwed up her face and held up her hand. "I'll go and warm up your plate."

Lizzy laughed and followed her into the living room. She immediately noticed that something was different. The room seemed somehow fresher, warmer, and more welcoming than it had yesterday. It took her several seconds to realize that the place had been given a really good cleaning. She felt something inside her stir. Maurice had always been the one to show initiative when it came to cleaning up the place. She'd let Lizzy off the hook as long as she *cooperated*. Lizzy had been the one who had done most of the designing when they had bought the place, but it had been Maurice's daily touches that had made their home warm and welcoming. She remembered the first time they had had to spend a week away from one another. Lizzy had missed her the whole time and she had come home late in the night to find Maurice still up, waiting for her.

Maurice was barely up from the couch before Lizzy bridged the distance and took her in her arms, kissing her long and hard. She managed to whisper, "I love you," but the words did not do justice to what she felt. She needed Maurice in every possible way. Maurice broke free from the kiss and stared into her eyes, looking farther than anyone else ever had, and whispered back, "I love you too."

Lizzy had made love to her right there on the couch. It had been quick and rough, her urgency too strong for her to go slow, and Maurice had surrendered to her, giving herself completely, knowing and understanding her need. With every kiss, with every touch, Lizzy had claimed Maurice as her own again and had felt with awe the woman she loved and respected climax under her fingers.

"Lizzy, are you okay?"

Lizzy ignored the voice that barely registered above the loud beating of her heart and closed her eyes, trying to hold on to the image of Maurice, ignoring the ache inside her chest. She felt a slight touch on her arm and knew instinctively that it wasn't Maurice. She opened her eyes again and for a moment lost herself in the warmth of Judith's gaze, finding a place free from Maurice and herself. A place that was so far away from her past and her pain that it had a soothing effect. Then her brain started processing again and she became acutely aware of how close Judith was. She broke eye contact and moved around her. She headed for the kitchen, unsure why, and automatically reached for the kettle, grateful to be able to touch something so meaningless. She could feel Judith watching her. Reluctantly, she took a deep breath and looked up. "I'm sorry."

"Lizzy, what just happened?"

Lizzy didn't know how to answer. What she felt was so private, so intangible, and ran so deep that she simply couldn't explain it, but to simply brush it aside was just too painful. Her own silence was deafening.

"I'll warm up your dinner." Judith's tone was even, but Lizzy detected no hint of judgment and simply stepped aside when Judith joined her in the kitchen. Food was now the furthest thing from her mind, but she remained silent as Judith set about warming up her dinner, grateful she wasn't pushing the matter.

"Why don't you go and sit down and I'll bring you your plate."

"You don't have to—"

"I know, but I want to. Now please go and sit down." Judith took the kettle out of her hands and turned to the sink to fill it. Not knowing what else to do, Lizzy did as Judith had asked. She sat in her favorite spot next to the fireplace and looked about her. She hadn't changed anything in the apartment since Maurice's death and yet it no longer looked the same. Without Maurice their home had lost its heart, and right now she felt completely detached from it. She focused on Judith as she worked in the kitchen and remembered how much she'd enjoyed shopping for Emily's costume with her and why she'd been eager to get home. Somehow, having something new to hold on to helped.

A few minutes later Judith passed her a plate of pasta and a mug of steaming tea. The words *thank you* seemed somehow insufficient, but she muttered them anyway for want of anything else to say. She still didn't feel like eating but forced herself to take a bite. The food was soft, creamy, and tasty, making it easy to swallow.

Judith sat on the other couch and watched Lizzy take a second bite. She wasn't sure what had just transpired. Lizzy had frozen on the spot and she'd gone to her, unsure what to do. She had searched Lizzy's eyes, trying to understand. She had never believed the notion that the eyes were the windows to the soul, but Lizzy's definitely told a story and she wished she knew a way to reach out to her. Lizzy was looking more like herself again, but Judith knew that whatever it was that held Lizzy captive still lingered just beneath the surface.

She wanted to ask her about it, she wanted to find a way in, but knew instinctively that now was not the right time and that maybe it never would be.

Lizzy placed her empty plate onto the coffee table. "How on earth do you do it?"

Judith felt a little self-conscious. She still couldn't believe that Lizzy liked her cooking so much. "Salt and pepper. They're the remedy for every meal."

"I'm sorry I didn't make it back on time last night. I did try."

"Don't move!"

Lizzy watched with bewilderment as Judith dashed out of the room. When she came back she was carrying Emily's costume and a roll of wrapping paper. She placed everything down onto the coffee table and then stepped back with a glowing smile.

"I was thinking we could give Emily her present now."

"But she's asleep."

"Exactly. That way we can put it at the end of her bed without her knowing and she can wake up to the surprise."

Lizzy loved the idea, and together they gift-wrapped the costume along with the accessories. Then they crept into Emily's room and placed the items on the end of her bed. They both stood back admiring their handiwork. Judith was contemplating whether or not she should tell Lizzy how much it meant to her to be able to share this moment with her when Lizzy whispered in her ear, "The place looks great, by the way. Thank you."

Judith had at one point in the afternoon wondered whether Lizzy would notice her attempt at cleaning the place up, but hadn't given it a second thought since. Realizing now that she had noticed her efforts and appreciated them gave her even more pleasure, and she was glad she had taken the initiative. She turned to face her and found Lizzy looking at her in a way that made her feel warm inside. "You're welcome."

She followed her out into the hall, making sure to leave the door open a crack. In the shadows of the hall, Lizzy spoke hesitantly.

"I was wondering if you wanted to watch a movie tomorrow night. I probably won't be back till late, but as tomorrow is Saturday, I thought I could pick one up on the way home."

Judith couldn't think of anything else that she would rather be doing tomorrow night and readily agreed.

❖

The following morning Lizzy was woken up by a mini pirate jumping up and down on her bed. Still half dead to the world, she let herself be dragged out of bed and somehow mustered up the energy to play with her until Judith came to her rescue. She then quickly showered and dressed and was about to leave for work when Emily joined her in the hall and asked her, with bright beaming eyes, if she could come back home before Emily went to sleep so that they could play more pirates. Lizzy didn't want to disappoint her, but she knew there was no way she was going to be able to make it back before Emily's bedtime. She tried as best she could to explain why she couldn't, which wasn't easy as it meant watching her eager smile fade away. Then Emily's eyes lit up again as she pleaded with Lizzy to promise her that no matter what, she would make it back on time Monday to hear about the audition. Lizzy felt powerless against Emily's charm, and not wanting to disappoint her, promised she would.

❖

She'd been able to keep to the shooting schedule over the weekend, but today was proving more difficult, and it was because of her promise to Emily that Lizzy was starting to lose her patience with the man standing in front of her. Time was ticking on and he was intent on explaining to her how he thought his character should act in a particular shot. Normally Lizzy would find the time to listen to any input if it meant a chance of making the scene better, but this man was obviously misinterpreting the function of his character and grossly overestimating its importance. It was moments like these when she wished she had it in her to be a little bit more ruthless. Instead, she held on to her patience and dug deep into her bag of people skills and managed to convince him to do what he was supposed to do, willingly.

As soon as she could steal a moment for herself she checked her cell to see if she had missed a call from Judith. She had arranged with her that she would call her as soon as she knew anything about Emily's audition, but Judith hadn't called yet and it was already nearly six o'clock. She'd felt anxious for Emily all day, wondering how she was doing and hoping that Mrs. Bouwman would at least let her do the audition even if she wasn't going to change her mind about Emily being a fairy. She decided she couldn't wait any longer to find out and found a spot that guaranteed a little more privacy and called home. She didn't even wait for Judith to finish saying her name.

"Did she make it?"

Judith giggled and whispered. "I'm not allowed to tell you. She wants to tell you herself. She said she'll wait up all night if she has to."

Lizzy couldn't help but grin.

Judith spoke a little more hesitantly this time. "Do you think you'll be able to get home in time?"

Lizzy rubbed the back of her neck feeling guilty, because she knew it would take a miracle.

"I'm not sure, but I'm doing my best."

Lizzy wasn't quite ready for the conversation to end. Somehow Judith's warm voice was a soothing antidote to her busy surroundings, and she wished she had the time to talk longer. She reluctantly hung up, even more determined to get the next scene done so she could get home.

❖

Judith welcomed her home with a warm smile.

"Is she awake?"

"She's awake, barely."

Lizzy instantly relaxed. "Can I go to her, then?"

Judith's smile deepened. "Of course."

Lizzy didn't need any more encouragement and set off down the hall to Emily's room and gently knocked on the open door. Emily answered sleepily. "Is that you, Lizzy?"

Lizzy pushed the door further open and stepped inside Emily's bedroom. The look of sheer delight on Emily's face made her heart melt.

"Hey, matey, so how did it go?"

Emily jumped out of bed and into Lizzy's arms. "Oh, Lizzy, I made it. I made it. I'm a pirate!"

"You did? That's brilliant!" Lizzy felt a surge of pride.

"You should have seen me, I was great…"

Lizzy sat on the edge of the bed while Emily recounted and reenacted every single detail of her audition. Judith entered at some point with a cup of tea for Lizzy and then joined them on the bed. Only when Emily had exhausted the story to the extent that little details were starting to change did Judith insist it was time for her to go to sleep. Emily insisted that Lizzy stay and tuck her in as well, and so Lizzy did.

Lizzy shook her head. "I can't believe she actually did it. I would have felt really bad if she hadn't." She followed Judith into the kitchen.

"I know, I can't believe it myself." Judith turned around and stopped laughing when she saw how Lizzy was looking at her. "What?"

Lizzy shrugged. "It's nice seeing you like this."

"Like what?"

Lizzy seemed to struggle for the right word. "Happy?"

"Seeing my daughter happy makes me happy."

"Well, it suits you."

Judith blushed and Lizzy immediately wondered why she'd said such a thing. She quickly looked away.

"Have you ever thought about having a child of your own?"

Lizzy felt very uncomfortable with the question. "I've never thought of myself as parent material."

"I think you would make a great parent."

"What makes you think that?"

"Because you're sincere in your interest and you keep your word."

Lizzy frowned. "That's not exactly the same as raising a child twenty-four seven."

"No, but believe me, it can make all the difference. Emily was looking forward to telling you her good news herself. She would have been crushed if you hadn't made it back, but you gave her your word and you kept it."

"Well, she did have a sword in her hand at the time she made me promise her."

Judith simply smiled. "Do you want to watch a movie?"

Lizzy was surprised at the question as well as the sudden change of subject.

"Considering there was a good chance you were going to be home early tonight, I took the liberty of renting one."

"I've turned you into a tea drinker and a movie watcher. I wonder what will follow next."

CHAPTER SEVENTEEN

Judith sat quietly in the passenger seat while Lizzy spoke into her cell phone. They had already dropped Emily off with Chris, who had been kind enough to offer his services as babysitter, and were now on their way to the studio. Judith had been looking forward to this day all week and although she felt excited, she was also feeling apprehensive. Not only was she about to find out where Lizzy went every day and see how a movie was really made, she was about to meet the people with whom Lizzy spent so much time. She felt nervous about what they would make of her.

This past week she had seen very little of Lizzy. Now that she was feeling well again, it was no longer necessary for Lizzy to play taxi for Emily except for on Wednesday afternoons while Judith worked. This meant that she didn't get to see her during the day anymore, and by the time Lizzy got back at night, Judith would already be in bed asleep. She'd missed seeing Lizzy for those short intervals.

They drove into an inner courtyard of an old-fashioned brown stone factory where an assorted amount of cars ranging from old Escorts to a new Chrysler were parked haphazardly. As soon as they were parked, Lizzy hopped out of the car and opened Judith's car door for her. Judith appreciated the gesture and would have thought it courteous if Lizzy hadn't still been talking distractedly into her cell phone.

"David, I am no more than a few feet away, but I'm going to have to hang up to open the door."

David was still talking when Lizzy flipped her cell phone shut and reached out to pull open a heavy wooden door.

"I'm sorry about that."

"Don't be. You're just doing your job, right?"

"Yeah, but I know how annoying it can be when you're with someone who is always on the phone."

"It's fine, Lizzy, really."

Judith followed her down a narrow corridor and into a room she guessed, from the tables and chairs and the empty white plastic coffee cups spread about the place, to be the designated cafeteria. Before they could take another step, two men, who were seated off to the right, immediately got up and approached them, engaging Lizzy in conversation. Judith stood quietly next to her and listened as Lizzy calmly answered their questions. Then she felt Lizzy's hand on her arm, gently guiding her around the two men toward a makeshift counter on the far side of the room where a woman wearing a pair of blue overalls was buttering slices of bread. Judith noticed the woman give her the once-over before turning her attention fully on to Lizzy.

"Hey ya, boss, ready for the onslaught?"

"As always, Laura, and you?"

The woman motioned to all the coffee cups left abandoned. "My onslaught started more than an hour ago."

Lizzy turned to Judith. "Judith, this is Laura, our caterer."

Judith held out her hand. "Nice to meet you."

"Laura, this is Judith, a friend of mine."

"The pleasure's all mine, I'm sure."

Judith shook Laura's hand, but felt that Laura held her hand a little too long.

"Judith was curious about how we make our movies, so—" Somebody called out Lizzy's name, causing her to glance over her shoulder. A slim, redheaded woman carrying a pile of paper had just entered the cafeteria.

"Look after her for me, Laura, will you? Make sure she's okay?"

"No probs, boss, sure thing."

Lizzy turned to Judith, her voice softening. "You'll be all right with Laura. If you need anything, just ask her."

The redhead joined them and cleared her throat. Lizzy smiled and rolled her eyes, already stepping away. "You're in good hands. I'll see you later."

"So what will it be, tea or coffee?"

"Hmm?"

Judith tore her eyes away from Lizzy's receding back and found Laura looking at her in a way that made her feel very self-conscious.

"Coffee, please."

Laura started filling a plastic cup with coffee from a big metal canister.

"So you and the boss are just friends?"

Judith didn't know what to make of the question, considering Lizzy had only moments ago introduced her as one. She accepted the cup of coffee Laura held out for her and first took a sip before answering, "Uh-huh."

"Well, you must be some friend. She's never brought anyone with her on set before, and I know quite a few gals that would just kill to be her *friend*." Laura wriggled her eyebrows and for a moment Judith was unsure whether she had understood Laura's implication correctly, but before she could question her about it, a voice sounded out through an intercom announcing that shooting would start in ten minutes.

Laura's attitude changed. "Hey, I best get you settled before it's too late. Come on."

Judith followed her through the doorway Lizzy had disappeared through only a few minutes earlier and was immediately taken aback by the view. They were standing inside a great factory hall, and right in the middle of it was a life-sized interior of an old Victorian house. Huge lights beamed from all around, and cables and wires crisscrossed over the floor like a never-ending labyrinth of snakes. People in modern dress walked among others who looked like they had just stepped out of a Charles Dickens novel.

Judith was struck by the authenticity of the décor. She whispered, "It's beautiful."

Laura grinned. "Yeah, Lizzy's a sucker for details."

Judith didn't respond, but followed Laura along the right side of the factory wall until she stopped at an alcove filled with chairs and equipment.

"If you sit here you'll be able to see most of everything that's going on without getting in the way."

The chairs looked antique and Judith was hesitant to sit in one.

"It's okay, they're fake and won't break."

Judith chose one and tentatively lowered herself into it. She felt relieved at the solid wood beneath her.

"If you want more coffee or something, just walk back the way we came, but try to avoid moving about while the camera is rolling."

"Aren't you staying?"

"Nah. I've got lunch to prepare. Catch you later."

Laura left and Judith looked around for a sign of Lizzy. She spotted her standing in a far corner talking to two men. She recognized them as being the same pair that had accosted them at the door when they had first arrived. She sipped her coffee and watched them. Both men spoke animatedly, their hands flying through the air. Lizzy seemed more composed and her hand movements more precise. Judith found her captivating to watch. It seemed a decision had been made, because one of the men raised his hands in a manner of defeat while the other ran off, all geared up. Lizzy tapped the remaining man on the shoulder, saying something to make him smile. Judith felt a jolt of excitement as Lizzy looked up, straight at her. Surprised at the unexpected feeling, she hesitantly lifted her hand and waved. Lizzy waved back and started toward her.

"Are you all right here?"

"I thought you said that you only directed on a small set."

Lizzy smiled. "This *is* small compared to most." She sat in the chair next to her and stretched her legs, which puzzled Judith.

"Shouldn't you be doing something right now?"

"I am." She reached into the pocket of her jeans and pulled out the car keys. "I have about sixty seconds left before my day really starts, and I don't have a true indication of how long it's going to be."

Judith gently pushed Lizzy's hand away. "I'll wait for you."

"What if you get tired or bored?"

"I won't."

Lizzy frowned. "Would you take them anyway, for my peace of mind?"

Judith looked into Lizzy's eyes and felt compelled to give her what she wanted. She held out her hand. "Forget about being a movie director, you should have been a negotiator."

Lizzy dropped the keys into her palm. "You'd be surprised how much of a negotiator a movie director has to be."

❖

Judith watched in awe as everybody worked, especially Lizzy. She witnessed the patience she was accustomed to seeing, but she also saw competence and what she could only describe as creative strength. The way she directed people, crew and actors alike, the way she took a moment to think, the look of sheer concentration on her face and the way others listened to her. Judith knew she had no right, but she couldn't help but feel a little proud of her.

She had been so engrossed in watching Lizzy at work that she had lost track of time and was surprised when Laura approached her suggesting that she join her in the cafeteria before the whole gang swooped in for lunch. Just as Laura was dishing her up a plate of sandwiches and a bowl of vegetable soup, lunch was announced over the intercom, and it wasn't long after before the cafeteria was swarming with women and men munching on sandwiches and slurping up soup.

Judith had kept an eye on the doorway waiting for Lizzy, but when it became apparent that Lizzy wasn't coming she got up to ask Laura if she knew where Lizzy was. Laura explained that Lizzy rarely came into the cafeteria at lunchtime. Judith asked her if Lizzy actually ate at lunchtime, to which Laura shrugged and said that she figured Lizzy was old enough to look after herself. "She knows where the grub is."

Judith didn't like the idea of Lizzy working on an empty stomach and knew her well enough by now to know that that was exactly what Lizzy would do. Annoyed at Lizzy's irresponsibility toward herself and Laura's complacency in the matter, she picked up another plate of sandwiches and headed back into the big hall in search of Lizzy. She found her sitting on a couch with a beautiful dark-skinned woman inside the fake Victorian living room. Judith had noticed the woman earlier when she had been watching everybody at work. She had stuck out from the others not only because of her stunning looks, but because there was an earthliness to her that Judith found commanding. She was tall and slim, but powerful in her stride and elegant in her hand gestures. Her hair was braided and wound artistically around her head. Her clothing was colorful but chic.

They were engaged in conversation and Judith noticed how close they were sitting next to one another and how comfortable they looked. The picture surprised her, because Lizzy had always given her the impression that she didn't like people getting too close to her and Judith had always tried to bear that in mind. She felt silly for bringing the sandwiches and turned to leave when the other woman noticed her.

"Can we help you?"

Before Judith could answer Lizzy quickly rose. She no longer looked comfortable. "Anita, this is Judith. Judith, this is Anita."

Anita's smile was striking and she gracefully offered Judith her hand. "Judith, I'm pleased to meet you. Why don't you join us?" She gestured to the couch were they had just been sitting.

Judith nervously waved the invitation off. "Oh no, I didn't mean to disturb you, I just thought you might be hungry." That last bit she directed at Lizzy.

Anita looked back and forth between them and jabbed Lizzy in her side. "This is when you say thank you."

Lizzy took the plate Judith held out and mumbled a thank-you.

Anita frowned at her before speaking to Judith again. "You should join us, Judith. We were just about done with our little talk anyway."

It was obvious that Lizzy felt uncomfortable and that it was her presence that was causing it. Feeling a little hurt, Judith shook her head and smiled politely.

"Thank you, but no. I don't want to keep you from your work. It was nice meeting you, though." She shook Anita's hand one more time and then turned and headed back to the cafeteria. As soon as Judith was out of earshot, Anita stepped in front of Lizzy and spoke firmly. "What was that all about?"

Lizzy avoided eye contact. "How do you mean?"

"Well, you weren't particularly your usual charming self. Were you worried about me meeting her?"

Lizzy shrugged. She'd known that by bringing Judith to the studio it was inevitable that they would meet, and she'd been fine with that idea until that moment had arrived. Her initial delight at seeing Judith standing in front of them had instantly disappeared when she realized she was about to meet Anita and she'd suddenly felt extremely nervous. Anita's tone softened. "Is she becoming more than a friend?"

"No, of course not."

Lizzy was surprised by the sharpness of her own voice and felt even more awkward. Anita studied her for a moment before taking the plate from Lizzy's hands. She walked back to the couch and spoke matter-of-factly: "Well, just so you know, I like her." She bit into a sandwich and spoke through a mouthful of cheese and tomato. "Are you just going to stand there?"

Lizzy remained standing a few moments longer, unsure what to do with herself. She hadn't meant to snap at Anita or be impolite toward Judith, and she felt crap about having reacted that way. She joined Anita on the couch and picked up a sandwich. She took a bite, grumbling, "You don't even know her."

"If she cares enough to worry about your stomach, that's all I need to know."

❖

Judith had watched Lizzy work for most of the day, but after lunch her heart had been less in it. Lizzy would glance up every now and again and smile in her direction, but knowing that her presence had made Lizzy feel uncomfortable around her friend had put a damper on her enjoyment. After the dinner call she had stayed behind in the cafeteria to help Laura clean up and they had ended up chatting about Laura's plans to open up her own restaurant. It was eight o'clock when it was finally announced over the intercom that they were stopping for the day and everybody was asked to gather in the cafeteria. Laura expressed her surprise at the announcement and explained that it wasn't usual. They both stayed seated as the crew and cast started filing into the room, filling the surrounding tables. Anita and Lizzy were the last to arrive, but Lizzy stayed put just inside the doorway while Anita walked to the front of the room and asked everyone to be quiet.

"As most of you know, Sam and I have been seeing each other on and off for the past few years." She smiled affectionately in the direction of a tall, thin man close by. "Well, we've decided it's time we stopped messing about and finally settle down…with each other."

The room exploded with the sound of people clapping and cheering. The man whom Anita had smiled at got up and joined her, taking her hand. Judith thought the simple gesture sweet and looked back at the doorway to where Lizzy stood and found her looking straight at her. Lizzy immediately averted her eyes.

Anita waited for the room to quiet down. "Anyway, we've decided to throw an engagement party at my place next week Friday. Now, I know it's short notice, but we were scheduled to film that night anyway, so I know none of you have plans or prior engagements."

Again people cheered and Anita had to shout over the noise. "So there's no excuse for not being there."

People started to get to their feet to congratulate them personally and Judith was contemplating whether to go to do so herself when Lizzy spoke softly at her side.

"Are you ready to go?"

She was surprised that Lizzy would want to leave before congratulating her friend, but then quickly figured that she might have already known about the announcement and done so already.

Judith said a quick good-bye to Laura, wishing her luck with her future restaurant, and left the bustling cafeteria with Lizzy. They were just about to step through the big outer wooden door when Anita called out Lizzy's name from the other end of the hall. They both stopped and turned to face her.

"I knew you'd try to skunk off."

"I'm not skunking off."

Anita reached out and gently took hold of her arm. "I want you there, Lizzy."

She held Lizzy's gaze as if making sure the message got across before turning to face Judith. "And you're invited too, Judith. In fact, I insist you accompany my director here and make sure she turns up."

It was clear by Anita's words that she was convinced Lizzy would not want to go to her engagement party, and Judith wondered why Lizzy would not want to celebrate her friend's happiness. She wasn't quite sure how to respond and opted for the polite.

"Thank you. I'll look forward to it."

Anita smiled gratefully, then raised an eyebrow at Lizzy.

Lizzy rolled her eyes in response. "We'll be there."

"Good." Anita tapped Lizzy on the arm one more time, then walked away waving a finger in the air. "Friday."

❖

Judith let her head fall back against the headrest. It had been a long day and she was glad to be in the car on her way home. "How on earth do you do it?"

"Do what?"

"Keep track of it all?"

"By the time we start filming, the movie has already played itself off in my head a hundred times. For me, it's just a case of making sure that what I see in my head is in the camera lens when we shoot."

Judith watched the streets pass them by.

"Don't you approve of Anita's engagement?"

"What makes you think I don't approve?"

"Well, you didn't seem all that excited about it, and Anita seemed to be under the impression that you might not go to the party."

"I am happy for her. For both of them. It's just been a long day, that's all."

Lizzy sounded sincere and tired, but Judith knew instinctively that there was something Lizzy wasn't telling her. They turned off onto Chris's street and Judith decided to leave it be for the time being.

CHAPTER EIGHTEEN

Chris opened the door with his face covered in paint and frowned at their laughter, pointing out that he wasn't the one taking extra art classes. They followed him inside and found Emily sitting at the dining table with a mess of paints and brushes spread out in front of her. Her face was covered in paint as well.

Judith let out a long sigh. "What have you done to my girl?"

Chris responded with exaggerated dissent. "Don't you mean, what has my girl done to you?"

Lizzy patted him on the back and teased, "You've loved every minute of it."

Chris showed her his tongue. "So, are you two hungry? We ordered Chinese and there's plenty left over."

Judith pulled a tissue out of her pocket and started cleaning Emily's hands. "If you don't mind, I'd like to get this little one to bed."

"Well, take it with you. It'll only get thrown out otherwise. Tom doesn't like keeping takeout."

Lizzy followed him into the kitchen. "Speaking of the devil, where is he?"

"He's on the graveyard shift. You just missed him."

"Thanks for doing this today."

"No thanks necessary, I thoroughly enjoyed myself. In fact, feel free to call me whenever you need a babysitter."

Lizzy found it strange that Chris was telling her, of all people, that he was available for babysitting and yet she already needed one for next Friday.

"Well, we'll need someone for next week Friday, but I doubt you'll be free."

Chris looked up expectantly. "Is there something going on I don't know about?"

"Anita and Sam have just announced their engagement and they're throwing a party. I'm sure you'll receive your invitation in the next few days."

"Well, well. It's about time those two tied the knot. So, are you going?"

"I don't see how I can get out of it. Anita made it abundantly clear she wants me there." Lizzy paused. "She's invited Judith as well."

"Are you all right with that?"

Lizzy simply shrugged and Chris sighed. "I wish you'd talk to me."

"What do you call this?"

He smiled affectionately. "Bread crumbs."

Lizzy knew he was concerned about her and thought she needed to talk about how she felt, but she simply hadn't the words to offer him.

He held out the bag of Chinese for her. "Tom's got a niece who's always babysitting for people. I'll give her a call. Now come on, you need to get the ladies back."

Lizzy was fully aware of Emily dozing off in the backseat and Judith sitting next to her in the passenger seat holding the bag of Chinese food on her lap. Their presence felt familiar and reassuring, and yet that same familiarity frightened her. Up until a few months ago she hadn't even known they existed and now, somehow, they had become a part of her life. A life she had been convinced she no longer wanted. Among her feelings of anger and despair there had always been one thing she had known for certain: every day lived without Maurice was a day not worth living. But that had been before morning cartoons, pirate costumes, and home-cooked meals. She realized she was starting to enjoy things again, like watching movies with Judith and playing pirates with Emily, but how could she without Maurice?

By the time they got home Emily had fallen fast asleep, and because Judith already had her hands full, Lizzy had been the one to pick Emily up and carry her up the stairs. She had done it without thinking, but as she climbed the stairs she was struck by the vulnerability of the sleeping child in her arms and felt a profound sense of protectiveness toward her. She carried her to her bedroom and carefully laid her down.

For the past few years her home had been empty and cold, a mere memory of the warmth and promise it once held, but for the past few months her home had been filled with life and activity. The sleeping girl portrayed a vibrancy of life that was a startling contrast to the death and anger that held Lizzy captive. Lizzy felt confused and out of place. Judith started undoing the laces on Emily's shoes and deftly pulled the shoes off her feet. Lizzy found comfort in the idea that Judith knew exactly what she was doing and left the room leaving Judith to be the mother that she was.

Lizzy had already laid out the food on the dinner table and was pouring wine into glasses by the time Judith joined her. They started dishing up the food onto their plates and it wasn't long before Judith realized that Lizzy wasn't actually eating and that she was way off in thought.

"A penny for your thoughts?"

Lizzy looked up puzzled.

"You haven't said a word since we left Chris's."

Lizzy laid her fork down and rubbed her left temple. "I'm sorry. I don't mean to be unsociable. I've just got some things on my mind."

Judith wondered if her silence had anything to do with Anita's good news. Lizzy hadn't jumped with joy like the others had and she'd been withdrawn since. She'd believed her when she'd said she was happy for them, but she was convinced there was more to the story than what Lizzy was letting on.

"Do you want to share them? I mean, if it's a problem, they say two heads are better than one."

A problem... Lizzy had never thought of the void inside her as a problem. She'd simply accepted the torment of its presence as the natural effect of Maurice's absence. How did one share anger, frustration, and despair?

Although Lizzy's face revealed nothing, Judith sensed her distress and wanted to somehow help soothe it.

"You've helped me, maybe I can help you."

"What makes you think I need helping?" Lizzy retorted dryly.

Judith waited a moment before daring to continue.

"Because you're carrying something inside you that obviously pains you, and you don't seem able to talk about it."

"Why is it everybody wants me to talk? It's not like it's going to change anything, is it?"

Judith's first response was to cower from Lizzy's outburst of anger, but she heard the anguish and pain behind her words and tried to stay calm.

"Lizzy, please—"

"Lizzy please what? What, Judith?"

Judith could feel her own heart pounding faster. "Lizzy, you'll wake Emily."

Lizzy remembered Emily asleep, vulnerable and trusting in her arms. Regret swept through her, coiling itself around the rampaged emotions that clawed at her heart. She did the only thing left in her power to do: she walked away.

❖

Lizzy strode down the dark street oblivious to her surroundings until she reached the gates of the one place she had avoided for the past three years. Of course the iron gates were closed and padlocked, but Lizzy didn't hesitate. She pulled herself up and over, landing firmly on her feet on the other side. The only light was that from the moon and a few stars, but she walked purposefully past all the other headstones until she reached the one she had come for. She took a breath before kneeling and lifted her fingers to the engraving she knew to be there.

IN LOVING MEMORY

OF

MAURICE FERRIER

1974–2006

A DEVOTED SPOUSE,

A BLESSED GRANDCHILD,

A FAITHFUL FRIEND,

SHE LIVED IN LOVE

AND WILL BE

FOREVER IN OUR HEARTS.

Lizzy had refused to come here after the funeral, not wanting to accept that the woman she loved lay here, outside, in the cold ground. It had been too much for her mind to comprehend that the body she loved, the body that had once been warm within her embrace, was now cold and lifeless, buried among strangers.

She didn't know what to expect or why she'd come now, but as she ran her fingers over the words engraved into the cold headstone she realized that the part of Maurice she had really loved was not buried there. What Lizzy had loved had surpassed anything physical; it had been Maurice's soul, her every thought and emotion, her very essence, and that could never be buried or laid to rest in the dirt. Something so beautiful couldn't just disappear into nothingness. It had to exist, had to live on in some form or another. She sat on the cold ground, resting her back against Maurice's headstone, and closed her eyes. She remembered the dream she'd had where she had seen Maurice among the children in the orphanage. She watched her again, and as she did so, she felt her anger slowly start to subside.

❖

It was near dawn when she finally left the cemetery. She felt raw and tired and wasn't ready to face Judith. So instead of going home she headed straight for the studio. An invisible cloud hung around her all day, but she tried to stay focused. Judith's expression from the night before kept flashing to mind. Lizzy had acted completely out of character and she felt utterly ashamed of herself.

When she got back that night she found the apartment shrouded in darkness, and if it hadn't been for the rays of light escaping into the hall from Emily's bedside lamp, she would have sworn she was alone. She contemplated knocking on Judith's door to apologize to her, but she wasn't able to think of any words that would relay what she truly felt.

It was something one of the crewmembers said in passing the following day that gave her an idea. She knew it could backfire, but she needed to do something, anything, to let Judith know how sorry she was. So she made the necessary plans.

She left the studio just before seven and nervously opened her front door twenty minutes later. She found Emily sitting on the couch reading a book, but there was no sign of Judith.

"Hi, kiddo. Where's your mom?"

"She's running my bath."

Lizzy started doubting whether this was a good idea. Emily seemed to pick up on her dilemma.

"What's the matter, Lizzy?"

"I want to ask your mother to go somewhere with me later, but I'm not sure she will want to go."

"You'll never know if you don't ask her."

Lizzy couldn't help but smile at her down-to-earth response.

"Just say your mother agreed, would you mind if Chris came over to babysit?"

❖

Through the open bathroom door Lizzy could see Judith sitting on the edge of the bath, but she knocked anyway out of politeness before entering. Judith didn't even look up and Lizzy felt her courage quickly start to waver, but she commanded herself to continue before it completely disappeared.

"I was wondering if you'd let me take you somewhere tonight."

"It's a weeknight. I can't just leave Emily."

Judith still hadn't looked up and her tone of voice was flat. A big part of Lizzy wanted to turn and walk away, not wanting to have to deal with the guilt she felt, but she knew she couldn't.

"I've already called Chris and he said he would be prepared to come over and babysit. All I have to do is confirm it and he'll be right over."

She held her breath knowing this was crunch time and hoped that Judith would not take her persistence the wrong way.

Judith stood, wiping her hand dry on a towel. "Lizzy, if you don't mind, I'd rather be left alone."

Lizzy felt her heart sink with the weight of Judith's dismissive words and had no idea how to continue. Emily appeared at her side.

"I think you should go, Mommy."

Judith turned in their direction for the first time, obviously surprised to hear Emily. She looked back and forth between them until her eyes rested on Lizzy. Lizzy felt uncomfortable under their scrutiny, but she held her gaze and said the only thing that came to mind. "Please?"

Judith stared at her a few moments longer. "I suppose one of you should call Chris, then."

❖

They drove in awkward silence until Lizzy finally pulled the car into a parking space at the side of the road.

"We have to walk the last bit."

"Are you going to tell me now where you're taking me?"

"Ecuador."

"Ecuador, what's that?"

"It's the name of the university's movie theater."

"You're taking me to see a movie?" Judith sounded more confused than surprised.

"Not exactly."

Judith felt too tired to question her further. She'd worked hard all day and hadn't slept well during the two nights since their altercation. She wouldn't have come if it hadn't been for the look of sheer humbleness on Lizzy's face and Emily's determination. Lizzy's outburst had upset her, more than she cared to admit. It wasn't the outburst as such; it had more to do with the fact that Lizzy either didn't want to or was not capable of letting her in. She didn't understand why it bothered her so much and couldn't believe how quickly she had become emotionally caught up with a woman who she had met only recently. She had thought of nothing else for the past two days.

Lizzy led her down a side alley and stopped in front of a shabby door. She rang the bell three times, then waited until a ginger-haired man with a stubbly beard opened the door.

"Hey ya, Lizzy. It's been a while."

"It sure has been."

Lizzy shook his hand. "Thanks for doing this, Jacob."

"Well, like you said, I still owed you one."

They followed him up a small flight of stairs and entered a small movie theater. Everything, including the seats and walls, was covered in a velvety red material that looked tattered after years of wear.

"I've left you some snacks on the best seats in the house."

Lizzy shook his hand and thanked him again before he left them alone. Judith followed Lizzy down the small aisle and then down a row of seats until they reached the two seats filled with popcorn and the like.

Judith started clearing her seat. "I thought the best seats were supposed to be the most central."

"A lot of the time they are, but it always depends on the shape of the room and the positioning of the chairs and how the sound travels. In this place these are it."

Once they were seated Judith glanced around and furrowed her eyebrows as it dawned on her.

"Are we the only ones?"

"Yes."

For the first time in days, Judith felt uplifted. She hadn't been to a movie theater since her early teens and never before had she sat in one alone. The notion was exciting.

"So what are we going to see?"

"Flicks."

"What's it about?"

Lizzy smiled. "Flicks, as in old black-and-white silent movies."

Just then the lights faded and the screen flickered to life.

Two hours later they were outside again heading back to the car. The night sky was clear and the air crisp, but Judith didn't mind the cold. She'd thoroughly enjoyed herself. It had taken her a few minutes to get used to the quirkiness of the black-and-white, soundless movies, but after that she found the stories fully entertaining.

"What on earth made you think to bring me here?"

"I thought you might like it."

"Well, I did. I loved it."

They turned a corner and were now just a few feet away from the car. Lizzy seemed to draw in a deep breath.

"And I wanted to apologize for the way I reacted the other night."

Lizzy's apology sounded heartfelt and it touched Judith deeply. So much so that she felt compelled to keep the conversation lighthearted and pretend it wasn't that big a deal.

"You didn't need to go to this much trouble to do that, although I admit, I'm glad you did."

Lizzy stopped walking and turned to face her. "It's important to me that you know that I don't usually act like that and that I'm not accustomed to raising my voice."

Judith wanted to reach out to her, to touch her, but she knew well enough by now that her gesture might cause Lizzy to recoil. She had enjoyed her evening and her company and appreciated her apology too much to risk Lizzy putting up her barrier again.

"I know, and your apology means more than you can imagine."

CHAPTER NINETEEN

With her hair wrapped up in a towel and another wrapped around her chest, Judith stood at the end of her bed with her hands on her hips, staring at the clothes she'd thrown down. She'd been looking forward to the party all week, feeling a butterfly sensation in her stomach whenever she thought of accompanying Lizzy, but now, with only a few hours to go, her excitement had turned into anguish and she was seriously wondering if she shouldn't make some excuse to stay home. She knew that most of the people there knew Lizzy and she wanted to look her best, but she doubted whether she would fit in and she didn't want Lizzy feeling embarrassed for having entered the party with her. There was a gentle knock at the door and she knew it could only be Lizzy. Without another thought she called her in. Lizzy opened the door and then quickly averted her eyes.

"I…I was just wondering if you'd seen my black pants?"

"Yes, they're folded up and in that pile on top of the washing machine."

Lizzy looked uncomfortable. "You didn't have to do my washing."

"I know, but I figured if I'm doing ours, then a little extra on top wouldn't kill me."

"Well, thanks anyway." She moved to leave but then nodded at the clothes strewn about the bed. "I'm sure whatever you choose, you'll look lovely."

Judith felt her cheeks burn and was grateful that Lizzy closed the door behind her without glancing back. She sat on the edge of the bed wondering why on earth it pleased her so when Lizzy complimented her like that. She thought back to all the times Lizzy had seen her crying, puffy eyed, and simply put, looking a mess. She felt even more determined to look her best.

Lizzy paced back and forth waiting for Judith in the living room. She'd never been one to fuss about her appearance, and that evening she had quickly showered and put on a black pair of pants and an olive-colored shirt. Maurice used to complain how unfair it was how good she looked with so little effort. Unfortunately for Lizzy, it meant she was always the one waiting around with time to think.

She'd been dreading the party all week and her only source of comfort had been the knowledge that Judith would be there. Judith was the only one that hadn't known her before Maurice's death and would therefore be the only one there without certain expectations or presumptions of her. That comfort had instantly disappeared when she had stepped into Judith's room half an hour ago. Her blood had raced at the sight of her wrapped merely in a towel. It had been a long time since her body had reacted that way toward a woman, and always, always it had been Maurice. She told herself that it was just a normal biological reaction after not having seen a woman for so long, but as she watched Judith walk toward her now, wearing a simple, but very elegant light beige suit, with her auburn hair loose around her shoulders, her blood raced again.

❖

The taxi pulled up in front of a tall, modern apartment complex that was clearly upscale. They stepped inside a wide, well-lit foyer and crossed a white marble floor to reach the elevator. The smartness of her surroundings only added to Judith's nervousness.

"I didn't realize that Anita was so well off."

"Looks can be deceiving. This place cost her a ton all right, but she worked hard to get it, saving her money for years. What you see here is the fruit of determination and hard labor. I personally don't like this modern look. I prefer a bit of history in my walls."

"Me too."

A silence fell between them as they waited for the elevator to arrive. Judith's nerves were starting to get the better of her and as soon as they stepped inside, she felt compelled to fill the silence.

"It's been so long since I've been to a party."

"Same here."

Lizzy sounded tense and Judith realized she'd been so caught up with her own nerves that she hadn't stopped to think that Lizzy might be anxious too.

"Are you nervous?"

Lizzy started tapping her right index finger against her leg and seemed to chew on her words before answering. "Yes."

Judith wanted to take Lizzy's hand into her own to stop the nervous tic, but withheld the urge. "Why?"

Lizzy looked down at her feet. "Because I'm no longer the person they want me to be."

Judith was completely taken aback by her statement and had no idea what to make of it, but before she could get her to elaborate, the elevator came to a stop and the doors slid open.

The apartment was spacious, with a high ceiling and long extending walls, but at the moment it was jam-packed with jostling bodies. Lizzy leaned in close and Judith caught a whiff of her tantalizing perfume, a fresh, crispy scent that was somehow intimately alluring. She liked it.

"Shall I get us some drinks?"

Judith appreciated the offer, but didn't want to be left alone. "How about we both go?"

Lizzy nodded and they started to make their way through the crowd, but they only made it a few steps before somebody called out Lizzy's name. Suddenly they were surrounded by a group of people engaging Lizzy in conversation. Lizzy managed to introduce Judith to the group and she was given welcoming smiles and firm handshakes, but it was obvious they were only interested in Lizzy. One woman in particular stood out: a tall blonde in a tight red cocktail dress with a bulging cleavage. She seemed intent on holding Lizzy's attention by keeping her in conversation. Lizzy seemed not to mind and Judith started to feel like a third wheel. She was growing increasingly thirsty. Somebody tapped the tall blonde on her shoulder, causing her to look away, and Judith quickly seized the opportunity to speak to Lizzy.

"I'm going to find us something to drink."

She turned to leave, but Lizzy whispered, "Please don't."

It took her a full second to register the meaning of Lizzy's words and realized in that instant that Lizzy needed her. The notion rocked her to the core and she felt a surge of protectiveness. Her previous nerves and discomfort disappeared as she resolved to stand with Lizzy and help her get through the evening.

"Hey, Lizzy! Judith!"

They turned in the direction of Anita's voice. She was making her way toward them and appeared happy and slightly tipsy.

"How long have you been here already, and why aren't you holding any glasses? Come with me."

She quickly maneuvered them away from the tall blonde and led them through the rest of the guests to an expansive open kitchen. The surfaces were covered with trays of party snacks. Anita opened the refrigerator, grabbed a can of beer, and shoved it into Lizzy's hand before turning to Judith. "Judith my dear, what will it be, wine, beer, or something stronger?"

"Wine, please."

Anita filled a glass with red wine for Judith and topped up her own. Lizzy was studying the crowd with a somewhat pained expression.

"How many people did you invite?"

"I'm not sure. The cast and crew, family, of course, and I also sent an automated invitation to all the addresses in my e-mail account. Sam did the same... Speaking of him, I haven't seen him in a while."

"Maybe he saw how many people you invited and ran off."

Anita slapped Lizzy on the arm. "Stop complaining. You know as well as I do that these types of parties are good for business. You should be out there mingling and convincing potential investors with that charm of yours to give us their money."

Lizzy pulled a face, causing Anita to laugh.

"Ah, speaking of potential investors, I think I see Mrs. van Schelten, if I'm not mistaken." She grabbed Lizzy's hand, pulling her forward, and turned to Judith.

"There's somebody I need her to meet. It will be good for business. I promise I'll get her back to you as soon as possible." She started to walk away, pulling Lizzy in tow, but Lizzy stood firm and spoke to Judith.

"Will you be all right?"

"Will you?"

Lizzy's eyes wandered to somewhere over Judith's shoulder and lingered there for a brief moment before they slowly returned to Judith's face accompanied by a faint smile. "Thanks for earlier."

Judith didn't know why Lizzy found it so difficult being here and although she wanted to know why, it was more important, at that moment, that Lizzy knew she was there for her. "You're welcome."

Lizzy hesitated and Judith gently touched her arm. "I'm not going anywhere." She nodded in the direction of Anita, who was waiting patiently a few feet away.

"Now go and help your producer reel in her fish."

❖

As the evening progressed, Judith ended up chitchatting with several people. Some of them were interested in her, while others, once they found out what she did for work, quickly found a way to end the conversation and move on. Through it all, she kept her eye on Lizzy. Now and again Lizzy would look up from her conversation, searching the room until she found her. They would smile at each other before looking away again. Chris and Tom arrived sometime during the evening and Judith was grateful to have somebody to talk to whom she knew.

Toward the end of the evening Judith found herself seated on a couch having an engaging conversation with a woman who also had once taught art, albeit to adults. While they talked she noticed that Lizzy was dancing a slow dance with Anita in her arms. They were dancing pretty close to one another and Anita was whispering something in Lizzy's ear. Their intimacy made her stomach tingle. She quickly tried to rationalize what she was feeling, but the woman next to her followed her gaze.

"It's strange not seeing her with Maurice, isn't it?"

"Excuse me?"

"I'm sorry, I presumed you knew Lizzy. Everybody else here seems to, or..." She nodded in the direction of the tall blonde staring shamelessly at Lizzy. "Want to."

Anita's fiancé stepped forward, blocking their view.

"Would any of you ladies care to dance?"

The woman next to Judith answered first. "I've already danced with you tonight, Sam."

"Indeed you have." He turned his smile to Judith, but Judith politely declined.

"You'd be doing me a great service. It won't be long now before I'm no longer allowed to dance with another beautiful woman without being punished." He winked and Judith couldn't help but laugh. She was fully aware that if it wasn't for the alcohol swimming through her veins she wouldn't have found his remark that funny, but she let herself be pulled up off the couch and led to the designated dancing area. She glanced over one more time to where Lizzy and Anita were dancing before she let Sam take her in his arms. She couldn't recall ever dancing with another man besides Menno, and she was amazed at how comfortable she felt dancing with Sam. He kept an appropriate distance and was sincere and gentle.

After only a few minutes of dancing Anita abruptly broke their hold. "Let's swap."

Before she knew it, Anita was off with Sam and she was in

the arms of Lizzy. The easiness she had just felt dancing with Sam immediately disappeared, a sort of breathless tension taking its place. She had never danced with a woman before and she didn't dare look Lizzy in the eye. She couldn't believe what she was feeling. Lizzy's scent tantalized her and the gentle firmness of Lizzy's arms felt safe, yet arousing. To her own amazement she realized she wanted to be closer to Lizzy, she wanted her arms tighter around her. For a split second she dared wonder what it would be like to rest her lips on the scented part of Lizzy's neck. Just then Lizzy leaned forward and whispered, "You had nothing to worry about, you are the most beautiful-looking woman here."

Judith felt her stomach ripple with warm waves. Lizzy's compliments always enthralled her and yet she never truly believed them, but being so close to her and having her whisper one in her ear made the world a very different place. For want of not knowing what to say or do, she just held on and followed Lizzy's gentle but firm lead.

CHAPTER TWENTY

Judith was feeling slightly hungover as she tiptoed down the hall past Lizzy's bedroom. She wasn't sure if she was still in bed and was trying to be quiet just in case.

She'd awoken from a deep sleep and had enjoyed a few seconds of peaceful contentment before the memories of the previous night had come flooding back: Lizzy letting her know she needed her there, the blond woman shamelessly trying to get Lizzy's attention, and then the dance. She felt confused by the emotions the dance had evoked and embarrassed about the way her body had reacted. Last night she had tried to blame it on the alcohol, but now, just thinking about it caused a slight ripple in her stomach. As she pulled on her coat she saw Lizzy's jacket hanging on the coat rack and knew that meant she was still in bed. Feeling grateful that she didn't have to speak to her yet, she quietly closed the door behind her and set off to pick up Emily.

❖

Emily was in the guest room playing something called an Xbox. Apparently Chris's niece had brought it with her the previous evening and left it for Emily to play with some more. Emily had no objections to staying a bit longer while Judith had a cup of coffee.

"So, did you enjoy yourself at the party last night?"

Judith felt Lizzy's hand at the base of her back leading her around the dance floor and quickly pushed the thought away. "Yes, although it was difficult not knowing anyone there. And you?"

"Tom would have preferred staying home, but me, where there's music, food, and drinks, I'm enjoying myself."

Judith took a small sip of her coffee before asking the question that had been on her mind all the way to Chris's. "Who's Maurice?"

Chris's smile disappeared. "What made you ask that?"

"I overheard someone last night saying they still found it difficult seeing Lizzy without Maurice."

"Have you spoken to Lizzy about it?"

"No, we were both done in by the time we got back and we both went straight to bed."

"What is it that you want to know?"

Judith lifted her shoulders and spoke honestly. "I don't know exactly. I just wondered who he was. I thought maybe he was an ex-lover."

Chris opened his mouth to respond but then hesitated. He studied Judith for a moment and his expression softened.

"She. Maurice was a woman, and yes, they were lovers." He looked into his cup. "I personally always thought of them as soul mates."

Now it was Judith's turn to gape as her mind struggled to understand the meaning of Chris's words.

"Lizzy's gay?"

Chris frowned. "Is that a problem for you?"

"No, no, of course not. I just, well, I never expected it." The tall blonde who had been shadowing Lizzy all night came to mind and Judith quickly pushed the memory of her away. "So you knew her?"

"Yes."

"Is she the one that hurt Lizzy?"

Chris relaxed back in his chair and sighed. "In a way, yes."

"What happened?"

Chris frowned. "I don't think I'm the right person to be talking to you about this."

Judith appreciated his reluctance and respected his loyalty, but during the past few months she had caught glimpses of Lizzy's hidden pain and she'd wanted to reach out to her. If she could know what the cause of that pain was, then maybe she could understand her better.

"If you feel awkward then don't tell me, but I'm not asking out of some morbid curiosity. I'm asking because I care."

Chris contemplated her words and seemed to accept their sincerity. "She died. Three years ago."

Judith stared at Chris, too shocked to believe him. "How?"

Chris grimaced. "Leukemia."

Judith's heart plummeted even further. The words, "Oh God!" escaped her lips.

Chris quickly responded with disdain. "God had nothing to do with it."

Judith knew leukemia was a horrible illness and a terrible way to die. The fact that Lizzy had loved someone with leukemia and had then watched her die seemed surreal. Her mind spun as she tried to absorb this information. She knew how she had felt when her father had died and how much she missed him still, each day, but to lose a loved one, a soul mate—the pain was unimaginable.

"How old was she?" Judith knew her question was pointless, but she was still trying to understand, to comprehend what Lizzy had gone through.

"Thirty-one."

"Oh, Chris, that's just terrible."

Judith tried to imagine Lizzy living with another woman.

"What was she like?"

Chris smiled wearily. "I can honestly tell you that she was one of the nicest people you could have wished to meet." He poured more coffee into his own cup and sat back down. "Each year, on the anniversary of her death, a bunch of us go visit her grave and have a drink to celebrate her life."

"And Lizzy?" Judith felt her heart break thinking of what Lizzy must have gone through. *How on earth does someone get over something like that?*

"Lizzy doesn't come. I don't even think she's been back there since the funeral. I know it's been three years, but I don't think she's truly accepted Maurice's death." Chris shook his head. "For a while there, I thought we were going to lose her too."

Judith felt a flicker of panic. "How do you mean?"

"Well, after Maurice died she just seemed to give up. She locked herself away at home. Wouldn't pick up the phone or see anyone, not even her own mother. We were all scared she'd do something to herself. At one point I used my spare key to get in and I found her just sitting there on the couch staring out into space, completely oblivious to my presence. I had to shake her to get her to acknowledge me."

Judith tried to imagine the scene and wished she could have been there for Lizzy.

"She must have really loved her."

"She did. They were together for twelve years, and I think they would have gone on forever."

Judith thought about all the times Lizzy had avoided certain conversations and the times she had pulled away from her. Certain things about Lizzy's behavior now started to make sense, and it hurt Judith to think of the pain that Lizzy must feel every day.

"She's never mentioned her, not once."

"She never talks about her. I know that's not supposed to be a healthy thing, but as long as she's venturing outside and getting on with her life, I'm not going to question it. You should know that Anita was Maurice's best friend, and last night would have been extremely difficult for Lizzy. As far as I'm aware, it was the first party Lizzy has been to since Maurice's death and certainly the first time she had appeared at such a gathering without her."

Realizing what Lizzy must have been feeling last night tore at Judith's heart and she felt lost with the revelations into Lizzy's past. She had wanted to know the cause of her pain so as to understand her better and help ease it, but now that she did know, she knew she would never be able to comprehend. What Lizzy had gone through left scars too deep to ever truly heal.

❖

Lizzy waited patiently in her car until she saw Isabel slowly making her way up the street carrying a bag of groceries. She stayed seated a few moments longer, debating with herself whether she wanted to do this before finally stepping out of the car and crossing the street.

Isabel turned around, looking a little apprehensive at hearing Lizzy's approaching footsteps, but Lizzy simply reached for the grocery bag. "Let me."

Isabel stared at her for a long moment before letting Lizzy take the bag. "You always were well mannered."

She started walking again and Lizzy walked silently by her side until they reached her house. Nothing had changed in the past three years, and the familiarity of it made it seem like it was only yesterday since she had last visited Maurice's grandmother. They walked on through to the kitchen, which had always functioned as the main room of the house. Lizzy did as she was told and lifted the bag of groceries up onto the counter and then sat at the kitchen table while Isabel set about making some tea.

"So how was the party last night?"

"How did you know about that?"

"Anita was here a few days ago informing me of her engagement. She even invited me to the party, bless her. I told her that I've been trying to age gracefully. Going to a party and being the only one with gray hair, a bent back, and a walking stick would not help me in my plight." She waved a hand in the air. "And besides, she's bringing him around tomorrow so I can meet him."

Lizzy knew that Anita had kept in contact with Isabel, but she'd had no idea how close they had become.

"He's a good guy."

Isabel poured steaming water into two mugs. "She told me you were living with someone."

"It's not what you think. We're not together or anything like that. She was a friend of a friend who needed help. I'm just helping her out."

"You don't know what I think, dear, and you don't have to go on the defensive with me either." Isabel sat on the other side of the table, in the same chair she'd always sat in.

"I'm sorry. I just don't want you getting the wrong idea."

Isabel raised an eyebrow. "I see. And what would that be?"

Lizzy didn't reply, but simply stared at her mug.

"It's okay, you know, to have feelings for someone."

Lizzy looked up sharply. "I don't have feelings for her, for anyone."

"Would it be so bad if you did?"

Lizzy felt sick and quickly stood, regretting she'd come. She walked the few paces to the hall, but then stopped. She wanted to leave, but the familiar smells and surroundings brought back memories, vivid, happy memories. She couldn't just walk out on them, never.

"Lizzy, sweetheart, come and sit down."

Lizzy turned to face her. Isabel had aged significantly in the past few years, but her face was still soft and her voice just as firm. She joined her back at the table, unable to look her in the eye.

"I know you miss her, Lizzy. I do too. Not a day goes by that I don't think about her. Have you spoken to anyone about the way you feel?"

Lizzy shook her head. "Why is it that everybody wants me to talk about the way I feel? It's not going to change anything."

"Perhaps, like me, they think it might help."

"Help what? Help me to move on? Because I can't do it."

"You don't have to."

"She made me promise to go on."

"And you don't want that?"

Lizzy shrunk back. "I can't do it, I don't know how."

"What is it you want, Lizzy?"

Lizzy struggled to find the answer. "I want...I want...I miss her so much." Lizzy buried her face in her hands and burst into tears. For the first time since Maurice's death, she wept real tears.

Isabel went to her, pulling her to her chest, and held her tightly, whispering, "Oh sweetheart, oh sweetheart."

She held her a long time, until the tears started to run dry. Only then did she let her go. She made one of her special pick-me-up grogs, sweet with honey and a few drops of lemon and rum, and placed it in front of Lizzy before sitting back down again.

"Nothing can bring her back, dear. All we can do is pray she is safe in God's hands."

"I don't believe in God, you know that."

"I know, but you did believe in Maurice, didn't you?"

Lizzy frowned. "Of course I did."

"Then you have to believe that her death means more than just the loss of her."

"What can possibly mean more than her death?"

"That's not what I said. To this day I don't know where I found the strength to say good-bye to her. From the moment her illness was diagnosed I prayed to God to spare her life, if need be to take mine instead, but he didn't and I admit, I've struggled with my faith ever since." She reached over and took hold of Lizzy's hand. "Whether or not you believe in God or whether or not you believe there was a reason for her death, you have the power to give it meaning."

Lizzy simply stared at her.

"Lizzy dear, there is no such thing as moving on, not when it comes to losing a loved one. Once we've opened our hearts to someone, no matter what happens, a part of us will always belong to that person. We may find a way to go on with our lives, but it will never be as bright as it was when they were alive, but live on we must, for them if not for ourselves. We have to experience, feel, see, and touch the things they no longer can. For them, Lizzy. It's our last gift to them and ultimately to ourselves." She reached up and wiped away one of Lizzy's tears. "And maybe, just maybe, if we're lucky, we can find someone again who will dare to love us for who we are and if we're strong enough, let them bring a new type of light into our shaded world."

CHAPTER TWENTY-ONE

Judith stepped off the streetcar and started off in the direction of Miss Rossum's home wondering what Lizzy was doing at that very moment. She had only seen her once throughout the past week, and that had been when Lizzy had dropped Emily off for her on Wednesday. Lizzy had been in a hurry and they had simply exchanged quick polite hellos followed by quick polite good-byes. Judith had been grateful that the encounter was brief because after her talk with Chris, she had felt apprehensive about seeing her again. What Chris had told her was so personal that she felt it was deceitful to pretend she didn't know, and yet she didn't want to risk hurting Lizzy by letting her know she did know. She was also struggling to put her own feelings into perspective.

She couldn't quite explain what she had felt dancing in Lizzy's arms at Anita's party, and knowing that Lizzy had once loved a woman only seemed to add to the importance of understanding her own confusion. She could not deny that she had felt aroused, and just thinking about that dance brought butterflies to her stomach. She tried to push her thoughts to the side as she arrived at Miss Rossum's.

Miss Rossum opened the door before Judith had a chance to ring the doorbell and was clearly excited about something. "Judith, come in, come in. I have some good news."

Judith stepped inside wondering what on earth had her in such a tizzy. Miss Rossum barely gave her a chance to take off her coat before ushering her on through to the living room. She led her over to the dinner table where she had laid out a tray of coffee and a writing pad and indicated to Judith to sit.

"My nephew paid me an unexpected visit yesterday. I don't know if I've ever mentioned it, but he's a deputy principal at a local high school." She didn't wait for Judith to answer. "Well, he happened to mention that they were looking to fill a vacancy in their art department and I remembered you telling me that you wanted to get back to teaching, so I told him about you. Now he did say that the deadline for accepting applications had passed, but I've never been one to easily accept a no. I know he's been feeling guilty for not visiting me more often, you see, so I played the guilt card and persuaded him to accept your letter of application. There is one slight problem, though. He insists on having it no later than tomorrow. So I thought we could use this time to get on with it." She tapped the writing pad expectantly.

Judith was speechless. She felt a tremor of excitement but couldn't quite believe what she was hearing. "I don't know what to say."

Miss Rossum picked up the pen and held it out to her. "You don't need to say anything, but I do suggest you start putting pen to paper."

❖

Judith quickly made her way down the Korte Reguliersdwarsstraat and entered Van Dobben, one of the few remaining authentic sandwich shops in Amsterdam. With its white tiled walls and men in white aprons it looked more like a butcher's than a sandwich shop, but with an unimaginable wide range of sandwich spreads to choose from, it was considered by many locals as the best sandwich shop in town.

She waited impatiently while they prepared her sandwiches. She had managed to write her application in the hour and a half she would normally have spent cleaning with Miss Rossum, and all she needed to do now was to type it up and get it to Miss Rossum's nephew. She planned to pick up Emily from school and then head over to the library to type it up. She knew Lizzy wouldn't mind if she used her computer, but she had already decided that she wasn't going to tell Lizzy or anyone else about her stroke of luck. Not until she knew she had an interview, which was a long shot. Telling Lizzy would somehow make it more real, and there was no guarantee that this was going to lead anywhere. It was exciting, but she didn't want to get her own hopes up. She still couldn't believe that Miss Rossum had cared enough to do this for her. Whatever came of it, she was going to buy her the biggest bunch of flowers she could afford.

That night as she wrapped tinfoil over the plate of food she had prepared for Lizzy, it dawned on her that Lizzy had not eaten the last two meals she had made for her. She wasn't even sure if Lizzy had come home or not. She had been so preoccupied with her feelings all week that she had only noticed now. Her own feelings and confusion slipped into the background as she started to worry that maybe something was wrong. After all, no matter how late or tired Lizzy got, she always ate the dinner Judith left her. She was contemplating calling Lizzy on her cell phone to make sure she was all right when Lizzy walked in.

Lizzy smiled a little awkwardly. "Hi."

Judith said hi back and gestured to the plate in her hands. "Do you want this?"

Lizzy looked sheepish. "Erm…do you mind if we talk first?"

Judith felt nervous, but calmly put the plate aside and joined Lizzy in the living room.

A long silence ensued and all Judith could do was wait as Lizzy seemed to struggle to say whatever it was she was going to say.

"I've been seeing someone." Lizzy didn't look up, but merely stared at her shoes.

Judith had no idea what that was supposed to mean and waited in slight trepidation for Lizzy to elaborate. When she didn't, she was forced to prompt her. "Anyone in particular?"

"Grandma Isabel."

Judith distinctly remembered Lizzy telling her about her family one night after they had watched a movie together.

"I thought you said that your grandparents were deceased on both sides?"

"They are. Isabel isn't my grandma, as such." Lizzy shifted in her chair.

"There's something I need to tell you. I was once in a relationship with somebody…" She winced. "Maurice…she died."

Lizzy's revelation took Judith by surprise as she realized that Lizzy had decided to open up to her. She felt guilty for already knowing about Maurice and felt compelled to be up front with Lizzy. "I know."

Lizzy seemed surprised, then shook her head. "Let me guess, Chris told you."

"Oh. Lizzy, I'm so sorry—"

"What did he tell you?"

Judith wished now that she didn't know about Maurice. "That she was your lover. That you'd been together for a long time and… that she died of leukemia."

"Acute myeloid leukemia, to be precise. It's painful, it's degrading, and it's made even crueler by its treatment: chemotherapy, radiation therapy, immunotherapy…" She leaned back into the couch, closing her eyes. "At first we thought she had the flu. The flu, for Christ's sake. Six months later she was gone. Just like that. One minute she was fit as a fiddle, the next she was…" Lizzy's voice faltered, but she took a deep breath. "And you know what makes it worse? Even though she was going through an indescribable hell, she was thinking of me."

Lizzy's expression was a mixture of bewilderment and awe, but she seemed to resign herself, letting her head fall back. Judith waited patiently, her heart pounding away.

"I hadn't seen Isabel since the funeral. I think I saw her as a mirror to the past and I just didn't want to be reminded of it because I wanted to be in it. Does that make sense to you?"

"I think so."

"It's hard having to go on with a life that you no longer want. I think I was scared that seeing her would make it even harder, and I could barely cope with the burden of it as it was."

Judith had already felt deeply affected to find out that Lizzy had lost her partner, but it filled her heart with immense sorrow to realize that Lizzy found life to be such a burden.

"So what made you go see her now?"

Lizzy hesitated, but she could no longer run from the truth. She couldn't explain it, but she felt she needed to be honest with Judith.

"You, Emily, the warmth and life you've brought into my home, forcing me to confront myself and my actions."

Judith was speechless. She had had no idea that their presence had affected Lizzy so much.

Lizzy gave a short, dry laugh. "See, a week ago I wouldn't have been able to tell you all this." She quickly rose and walked over to the kitchen to pour herself a drink, but after a moment's hesitation, put the bottle back down and pushed the glass away.

"She's invited you and Emily to dinner. She insists on meeting you. I understand if you feel too uncomfortable with the idea."

Uncomfortable. Judith repeated the word in her head. Not only was the invitation completely unexpected, but there was no way she could make sense of its meaning in just the few seconds she had known about it, let alone muster up the feeling of being uncomfortable with it.

"Why?"

"Why what?"

"Why does the grandma of your"—Judith struggled to find the right word. Somehow the word *ex* didn't do justice to Maurice's memory, nor did any other words that came to mind—"Maurice, want to have dinner with me?"

"She said she wants to meet the people who are having such a positive influence on me."

The expression of puzzled indignation on Lizzy's face was endearing.

"Do you want me to meet her?"

"I admit, the idea does feel strange, but...yes, I think I'd like you to meet her."

❖

Today of all days, the streetcar that Judith and Emily normally caught back home from the school arrived fifteen minutes late. On top of that Lizzy had been held up at the studio and was late getting home too, but in spite of the setbacks they had all managed to freshen up before clambering into the car and were now standing on Grandma Isabel's doorstep only a few minutes late.

Judith felt nervous. Not only was she about to meet someone who played an important role in Lizzy's life, but she was about to meet the grandma of the woman Lizzy had loved and then lost. She still wasn't sure why Maurice's grandma wanted to meet her, but she was aware their meeting was significant to Lizzy. Lizzy had been quiet during the drive over and Judith could sense her nervousness, which only heightened her own.

Grandma Isabel opened the door and greeted them warmly. "Judith dear, I'm so happy you could make it."

Judith was slightly taken aback by her cordiality, but embraced her back.

"And you must be Emily." She reached out her hand, but Emily didn't shake it. She merely nodded shyly and moved closer to Judith. Judith was a little surprised at her sudden shyness. Emily had been looking forward to meeting Grandma Isabel and she'd been driving Judith mad with questions about her for the past few days. Grandma Isabel seemed impervious to Emily's reaction and warmly invited them all in, leading them to the kitchen.

She directed them to sit at the kitchen table, which had already been set, and had Lizzy pour them all something to drink while she checked the garlic bread. It still needed a few more minutes in the oven, so she sat down with them while they waited. Both Lizzy and Emily were quiet, which made Judith feel even more awkward, but Grandma Isabel had no trouble starting up a conversation. She seemed keen to get to know Judith, and although her manner was direct, her questions were unobtrusive. Judith found her easy to talk to and started to feel more at ease with her.

It wasn't long before they were comfortably eating a warm, rich, homemade stew with roasted garlic bread. Lizzy seemed to relax and started to join in the conversation more willingly and Emily slowly started to come out of her shell. She told Grandma Isabel about her part in the school play and how she had gotten it. Grandma Isabel directed a raised eyebrow at Lizzy when Emily mentioned in not as many words that it had been Lizzy's idea to do the exact opposite of what her teacher had wanted. Like everybody else, though, once privy to all the facts, Grandma Isabel was sympathetic to Emily's cause.

They were halfway through their meal when Grandma Isabel asked Judith about her work. Judith felt nervous again. She'd expressly refrained from telling anyone about her job opportunity because of her fear of it not leading to anything, but now that Grandma Isabel had asked, she felt compelled to spill the beans.

"Well, today I found out that I have a job interview for a teaching position next week."

Lizzy was so surprised she was momentarily speechless. It was Grandma Isabel who was the first to congratulate her.

"Judith dear, that's wonderful news."

Judith smiled sheepishly. "It doesn't really mean anything yet. I mean, I'm grateful for the opportunity, but the chances of me getting it, well, it is a long shot."

Lizzy found her voice again. "Of course it means something. It means you could be a teacher again."

"Mommy, does this mean you're going to be a teacher at my school?"

"No, sweetheart. The job I'm applying for is at another school."

"Well, I think this calls for a celebration. Lizzy dear, why don't you pop down to the cellar and bring up one of those wine bottles I keep for special occasions and then Judith can tell us all about it."

After dinner Lizzy and Judith insisted Grandma Isabel sit and relax while they tackled the dishes. Grandma Isabel eventually gave in, but instead of sitting turned to Emily.

"Would you like to help me feed a special bird, dear?"

"You have a bird? Like at the pet shop?"

"Oh no, I wouldn't dream of keeping a bird in a cage. All of God's creatures should be free. No, this bird lives in my garden."

"But lots of birds live in gardens."

"True, but this one is different. One day I found him in the garden and I realized he couldn't fly, so I started putting out food for him and he hasn't yet decided to leave."

Emily looked alarmed. "But what if a cat sees him?"

"Well, he's gone and built himself a little nest, hasn't he?"

Emily seemed to think this over before asking her next question. "But how can he build himself a nest if he can't fly?"

Grandma Isabel smiled. "Well, he still has the use of his legs and he's found himself a nice spot not too high up off the ground which he can reach with a few hops here and there. He's a very clever bird. So, do you want to help me feed him?"

Emily's eyes shone bright. "Yes, please."

Grandma Isabel pointed to a cupboard door. "That's where I keep his seed. Why don't you get that while I change my slippers."

Emily seemed proud to have been given the task and quickly got up from her chair.

While Grandma Isabel and Emily tended to the bird, Lizzy and Judith tended to the dishes.

Lizzy picked up another plate from the dish rack and dried it off with the dish towel. She was feeling happy for Judith and hoped that this opportunity panned out for her, but she also felt a little bothered by the fact that Judith hadn't told her about it until now, even though she knew Judith wasn't under any obligation to do so.

"Why didn't you tell me about it?"

Judith dipped another plate into the bowl of soapy water before answering. "Because it wasn't a sure thing. It still isn't."

Lizzy squinted. "Yeah, but you could have told me."

"I had planned to initially."

Lizzy placed the dry plate in the cupboard, wondering why this was bothering her so much. "So why didn't you?"

"I just…didn't want to disappoint you."

Lizzy stopped what she was doing. On the one hand it touched her to think that Judith cared for her opinion, but it also hurt her to think that Judith thought she would judge her like that. "Whatever made you think you could disappoint me?"

"I know, it's silly."

Lizzy touched Judith's arm. "Judith, when I look at you I see a remarkable woman, a woman I respect. A person can only be disappointed if they expect something, and I don't expect anything from you. I do, however, hope that you'll do whatever you feel you need to do to be yourself, and I want you to know that I support you in whatever that is."

Tears swelled in Judith's eyes and at that moment Lizzy wanted nothing more than to soothe them away. She realized how easy it would be for her to reach up and wipe Judith's tears away. She forced herself to take a step back before she did something she might regret.

An hour later they were putting on their coats, getting ready to leave. Judith thanked Grandma Isabel for the lovely dinner and offered her hand, but Grandma Isabel pulled her in for a surprise hug.

"It has been a real delight meeting you, dear. Feel free to come visit me whenever you like."

Judith was taken aback by the woman's warmth and was trying to think of an appropriate response when Emily stepped forward. "Can I come back again?"

Grandma Isabel bowed down as far as her old bones would allow and pulled Emily in for an even bigger hug. "Of course you can, dear."

As they stepped out onto the street, Grandma Isabel caught hold of Lizzy's arm and whispered in her ear, "They're good people, Lizzy. I wouldn't mind seeing more of them."

CHAPTER TWENTY-TWO

Judith had tried to be sensible by going to bed early, but she was too nervous to fall asleep. She eventually decided to take a break from trying and got up to make a cup of hot chocolate. The door to Lizzy's study was open and she could see Lizzy sitting at her desk working. Ignoring the urge to knock, she started to move away.

"Nervous?"

Judith stopped and turned back. "Just a little."

Lizzy smiled, pulled out a chair, and gestured to Judith to sit in it.

"Only a little?"

It was clear by the way Lizzy was looking at her that she didn't believe it for a second.

"Okay, I admit, on a scale from one to ten, I'm nearing double digits."

Lizzy's light laughter was enticing. "Do you want to practice?"

"Practice? How?"

"Simple. I'll pretend to be the principal and I'll interview you."

Judith felt self-conscious and waved Lizzy's offer off as anything but serious. "Don't be daft."

Lizzy lowered her voice. "Miss Hilford. Welcome. Would you like a glass of water or some coffee before we start?"

Judith burst out laughing at Lizzy's imitation, but Lizzy continued on. "Miss Hilford, would you be so kind as to tell me what is so funny?"

Judith realized that Lizzy meant for this to happen. So, biting down on her laughter, she shuffled herself into a better sitting position and put on her best face.

They practiced the interview for almost an hour, and by the time they were finished Judith felt more confident about her chances.

The following morning she got up early to give herself plenty of time to get ready, but she soon realized she would have to hurry if she was going to make it on time. She had no idea where the time had flown to. Maybe it was the redoing of her hair several times or the extra makeup touches, but whatever the cause, her time had run out.

Both Lizzy and Emily sat waiting patiently in the living room and both immediately stood when she walked in.

"How does this look?" she asked, unsure whether she wanted to hear the answer.

Emily and Lizzy answered in unison, "Great! Perfect!"

Judith waved her hands through the air. "I can't believe I'm so nervous."

"You'll be fine, you'll go in there and you'll let them see the real deal. You were born to teach, remember that, and you love it. Remember that too."

"But what if they ask why I left?"

"Tell them the truth. Taking time out to raise a child is nothing to be ashamed of. Don't feel guilty for it."

Lizzy looked determined and Judith felt comforted by her confidence.

Lizzy reached for her cell phone. "I'll come with you."

"What?"

"I won't come inside or anything. I'll just sit and wait in the car."

"But I don't know how long it's going to take, and what about your work? I know you're struggling to make it on time as it is."

"First off, I don't care how long it takes, and secondly…this is important."

Lizzy flipped open her cell to call Anita.

"I want to come too."

They turned to look at Emily, who looked just as determined as Lizzy did.

Judith smiled affectionately at her. "Sweetheart, you have school."

Emily's face turned resolute. "I want to come too."

Judith wasn't used to Emily being so stubborn, nor Lizzy, for that matter, and it touched her deeply that they both cared so much.

"Okay, but you have to go back for the afternoon, okay?"

Emily's face transformed smoothly into a big grin. "Okay."

Fifteen minutes later they pulled up outside the gates of Mendel High School.

Judith undid her seat belt but made no attempt to get out of the car. Instead she clutched her bag and stared out the window at the school building. Lizzy turned off the ignition and all three sat silent for a few long seconds. Emily was the first to speak.

"You'll be fine, Mommy."

Judith looked over her shoulder at Emily, feeling her love in the depths of her soul. Then she glanced sideways at Lizzy, wanting desperately to tell her to drive on, but Lizzy, as if reading her mind, undid her own seat belt with emphasis.

"Judith, you're a beautiful, smart, capable person, and you need to start believing that, because when you do, you'll make them believe it too."

Lizzy's words inflamed something deep inside her and before Judith could stop herself she reached over and touched the side of Lizzy's face. "You are so kind to me."

Then, without another word, she stepped out of the car, leaving Lizzy and Emily with nothing to do but watch her disappear through the school's main entrance and wait in anticipation.

It wasn't long before Emily was sitting on Lizzy's lap pretending to drive and asking when they could go and see Grandma Isabel again. Lizzy answered all her questions as best she could, but she couldn't quite get her mind off the way Judith's touch had made her feel. She still felt the warmth of it swirling in her stomach.

After forty-five minutes of waiting they spotted Judith coming out of the school's main entrance and waited nervously for her to reach the car. Judith wasn't even seated before Emily excitedly asked the burning question.

"Did you get it, Mommy?"

Judith closed the car door and let out a long sigh before answering.

"I honestly have no idea. They asked me so many questions. Like why did I leave education and why I want to come back and such. I felt overwhelmed and I'm sure they noticed how nervous I was. I was so thirsty, but I didn't dare try to pick up the glass of water they had offered me. They said they would call me within the next few days to let me know."

Several days passed without word about the job, and Judith grew more anxious. At work she welcomed every window and surface that needed cleaning. The physical demands somehow helped curb her nerves and she was grateful for the distraction. One morning, just as they were about to leave the apartment, Emily presented her with a form from school on which she was supposed to write down how many tickets she wanted for the school play. Judith quickly scribbled down "two" and then realized what she had just done. She had automatically ordered a ticket for Lizzy. She knew she didn't need to ask Lizzy if she wanted to go, because she already knew that Lizzy would want to see Emily in her moment of glory, but it was this fact that made her pause. In the past she would have been the only one interested in Emily, and she most definitely would have been going alone.

It felt good to be able to share such an important moment in her child's life with somebody who cared. It made her think about the friendship that had grown between them and what it meant to her. Her aim had been to get a job and work hard so as to be able to get a place for Emily and herself. That was still her goal, but at that very moment she couldn't help but feel a little sad. The idea of no longer living in this apartment felt strange, and she couldn't quite imagine a life in which Lizzy wasn't part of every day. She wondered if their friendship would remain or if it would dissipate once she left.

Chapter Twenty-three

While some of the crew set about rearranging the set for the next shot, Lizzy took a moment to check her cell phone and found she'd missed Judith's call. Cursing under her breath, she immediately called her back.

"Judith Hilford speaking."

"And?"

Judith giggled. "I got it."

Lizzy struggled to say something appropriate. This was what she had been hoping to hear but hadn't dared hope for, and only one word came to mind as the news sank in. "What!"

"I know, I can't believe it myself."

"That's great, that's just great, Judith. We should do something… celebrate."

"Well, after I tried calling you and got no answer, I called Chris. I just needed to tell someone, and he insisted we go for drinks later."

Lizzy looked over her shoulder at the changing set. "I have no idea how long I'll be."

"I told him that, but he said the bar he had in mind was open late anyway. He also said he was going to arrange for his niece to come over and babysit and to call him as soon as you get home."

Lizzy grinned. Chris had obviously got the whole thing sorted.

"Okay, I'll call you when I'm on my way and I'll call for a taxi when I know for sure what time that'll be."

"I'll be waiting."

Lizzy hung up feeling tremendously elated at Judith's good news and went in search of Anita, also needing to share the good news.

❖

The taxi dropped them off in front of the Blue Ball. It was a gay bar that opened its doors to all sorts. On the weekends it was difficult to get in because of the great live bands they somehow managed to attract, but during the week it was a cozy joint where patrons could sit privately in a booth or have a quiet dance or play a game of pool in the back. Lizzy had once been a regular, but she hadn't been back in years. She hoped that Judith wouldn't feel too uncomfortable.

Chris hadn't yet arrived so they ordered drinks and sat in a booth opposite each other.

"So come on, then, out with it. Give me the details."

Judith laughed at Lizzy's obvious excitement. "Well, it's fifteen hours a week spread over four days, leaving my Fridays free, and I'll be teaching grades nine, ten, and eleven. The woman I'm replacing, who's on maternity leave by the way, didn't teach twelfth grade, which I'm glad about, because I can gradually get used to being in front of the class again without having to deal with the responsibility of getting kids to pass their exams."

"It sounds great, Judith. I'm so happy for you."

"Yes, and apparently one of the other art teachers will be leaving at the end of the school year, and if all goes well with me I'll be allowed to stay on and I'll be given his hours."

"That's fantastic."

"Yeah, but it's scary, though, going back after all these years."

"Of course it is. Whenever someone starts a new job it's scary, but you'll be fine and the school obviously believes in you, otherwise they wouldn't have hired you."

"You're really good for my ego."

Their laughter was cut short by somebody calling out to Lizzy.

"Hey, Lizzy darling!" A tall, slender, exotically dressed woman approached them. "What's this? The first time I see you in ages and you're with another woman?" She put her hand to her chest. "You've broken my heart."

Lizzy smiled at her old friend and Judith looked at her with a mixed expression of curiosity and amusement.

"Judith, this is Jeanette. Jeanette, this is Judith."

Jeanette fixed her eyes on Judith and elegantly stretched out her arm to shake her hand.

"Nice to meet you, Judith."

Jeanette kept her eyes on Judith as she plumped herself down next to Lizzy, forcing Lizzy to move up.

"Now tell me, dear, what's the secret to this girl's heart?" She placed a hand on Lizzy's arm and waited for Judith to answer. Judith simply stared at Jeanette with an incredulous look. Lizzy felt embarrassed and decided it was time she beat Jeanette at her own game. She caught Judith's eye and winked before answering for her.

"Judith can cook."

Jeanette's head snapped around to face Lizzy. "You're saying I can't cook?" She slapped Lizzy's arm. "You should try one of my famous breakfasts." She wriggled her eyebrows, causing Lizzy to laugh.

"So there's that handsome smile I've missed." She turned back to Judith. "So are you two an item?"

Lizzy quickly answered the question. "No, we're friends."

"Pity. It would have been a great piece of gossip." She turned her attention back to Lizzy. "So when are you going to put me in one of your movies?"

"When are you going to learn how to act?"

"Girl, you're looking at the next Julia Roberts." Jeanette put on her best smile.

"Am I indeed?"

"You just don't recognize a prima donna when she's right in front of you."

"Is that a fact?"

Jeanette puckered her lips. "It sure is."

Just then a man walked past and Jeanette followed him with her eyes.

"Mm, mm, mm. You'll have to excuse me, ladies, while I go catch a fish for my supper tonight."

She turned and gave Lizzy a quick kiss on the lips and whispered tenderly, "It's good to see you out and about again, sweetheart."

She stood, waved at Judith, and sauntered off in the direction of the man.

Lizzy shook her head. "I'm sorry about that. She somehow always manages to make herself center stage."

Judith leaned in closer. "Is she a bisexual?"

Lizzy smiled knowingly. "No."

"Now I'm confused. This is a gay bar, but she's after a man?"

"Jeanette is a transsexual."

Judith's mouth fell open. "You're kidding me!"

"Nope."

Judith looked in the direction Jeanette had headed. "I would never have guessed."

Lizzy took a sip of her beer.

"Most people don't."

"But she's so…"

"Womanly?"

"Beautiful."

Just then Chris and Tom entered the bar and the conversation turned back to Judith's new job.

❖

It was after two when they finally left the bar, but Judith was feeling too happy and too tipsy for the night to end and suggested to Lizzy that they walk home instead of taking a taxi. Lizzy easily agreed. After they'd said their good-byes to Chris and Tom, Judith wrapped her arm around Lizzy's and they set off at a comfortable pace. Even in the middle of the night there were always people wandering the streets of Amsterdam. Except for a handful of locals and the few faceless figures lingering in the shadows, it was mostly small pockets of tourists enjoying the late hour of the city. Judith felt completely safe walking arm in arm with Lizzy and held her closer, enjoying the freedom and intimacy of their late walk as they strolled along the Westermarkt. They passed the Homomonument, a memorial commemorating those who had been persecuted because of their homosexuality. It was also an homage to those who fought for equal rights. The memorial lay directly on the water of the Keizersgracht at the back of the Westerkerk.

The Westerkerk, once considered the hallmark of Amsterdam, gave Judith the impression it was shielding the monument. The church had been built in the seventeenth century and had the highest church tower in Amsterdam. Judith remembered reading Anne Frank's diary in which she frequently wrote about the church. Anne could see the spire from her attic window and said the ringing of its bells comforted her.

They turned off onto the Prinsengracht and headed deeper into the more quiet area of the Jordan district, toward home.

❖

They clambered up the long flight of stairs to the apartment and then tumbled inside the hall laughing. Once inside, Judith leaned against the wall and closed her eyes, sighing with contentment.

"Thank you, Lizzy, for all of it."

When Lizzy didn't say anything she opened her eyes and found Lizzy looking at her in a way that immediately sent tingles down her spine, and before she knew what was happening, Lizzy kissed her. Her initial shock was quickly squashed by the overwhelming sensation of warm lips gently pressing against hers and she found herself opening her lips, deepening the kiss, pulling Lizzy in closer. Then she felt the tip of Lizzy's tongue and fire thundered through her body, causing an involuntary moan to rise from within her and echo deep in the back of her throat.

"Urm, excuse me?"

They both jumped. Chris's niece stood just a few feet away, smiling coyly, and Judith felt extremely embarrassed. She quickly turned away, unsure what to do with herself. Lizzy seemed to find some composure and approached the teenager and asked her, in a shaky voice, how much she owed her. While Lizzy paid her, Judith forced her wobbly legs to move and headed for her bedroom, closing the door behind her. She leaned back against it, lifting her fingers to her lips, where she still felt Lizzy's touch. A part of her mind told her that it hadn't happened, but her heart was still racing, proving it had. She tried to refocus her thoughts, but they were elusive, pushed to the outer corners of her spectrum by her body's reaction.

There was a knock and she jumped, her heart pounding faster as she listened to Lizzy's softly spoken words.

"Judith, are you okay?"

Her heart dictated she open the door and reach out for her, but she felt paralyzed to do so by the confusing fluster of emotion that held her captive.

Instead, she rested her head against the door and waited until she knew Lizzy was gone.

❖

It cost Lizzy an enormous amount of effort to concentrate on her work. Her thoughts kept wandering back to what had happened the previous night, and when they did, feelings of arousal and shame washed over her. She had no idea how it had happened, but it had and the intense feeling of desire she had felt for Judith last night had taken her completely by surprise. One moment she was looking into her eyes and the next she was kissing her, and when she felt Judith kiss her back, a fire had ignited inside her. Her mind had struggled all day to understand it. Maurice was the only one for her. She was the one who had made her whole, and yet last night Lizzy had wanted only Judith, and when Judith had not answered her through her bedroom door it had felt like a knife to her heart.

Lizzy had no idea what she was going to say or do when she saw Judith again, but when she finally made it home that night, she found the apartment shrouded in silence and darkness and her heart sank even lower. She didn't need to check their bedrooms to know they were gone. There was a note on the kitchen counter, and for a moment she considered not reading it.

Dear Lizzy,

> *I've arranged for Emily and myself to stay at a hotel. I know you deserve more than a note and it is not my intention to hurt you, but I need some time to myself, and after last night I think this is best.*
> *I truly am sorry.*

Judith

Lizzy stared at the note, unable to think or feel. As quickly as they had come into her life, they had left.

CHAPTER TWENTY-FOUR

Lizzy rang Chris's doorbell, hoping he was still up. He opened the door in his pajamas and was clearly surprised to find her standing on his doorstep so late at night.

"Have you got a moment?"

Chris stepped aside to let her in. "For you, always." He led her into the living room. "Is something wrong?"

Lizzy walked over to one of the tall windows and looked out into the night sky. Chris sat down and waited patiently for her to answer.

"Judith's left."

Chris looked surprised. "She never mentioned anything about leaving last night. Did she find herself a cheap flat or something?"

Lizzy rubbed her forehead. "She's checked herself into a hotel."

"Why on earth has she gone and done that?"

Lizzy lowered her head. "To get away from me."

Chris shook his head in confusion. "I don't understand. I thought you were getting on. Even Tom noticed how happy you both were with each other last night."

Lizzy slowly moved away from the window, sat in one of the armchairs opposite Chris, and nervously tapped her fingers on the armrest.

Chris leaned forward. "What is it I'm missing here? What's happened?"

Lizzy inhaled a deep breath. "We kissed."

Chris's mouth dropped open. "You mean, really kissed?"

Lizzy simply kept tapping away.

Chris stammered. "When? I mean how…"

"Last night, and I'm not exactly sure."

"Do you want to tell me what happened?"

"One minute we were talking, the next…" Lizzy shook her head and closed her eyes.

"Did it go any further?" Chris asked tentatively.

Lizzy quickly stood. "No." She walked back to the window. "God, I wish it had never happened." She rested her head against the windowpane. "The apartment is so quiet, Chris."

"Do you love her?"

Lizzy responded agitatedly. "I don't know what I feel."

Chris leaned back in his chair, obviously needing a moment to process what she was telling him. "Have you tried contacting her?"

"Why would I do that? She left. She's made it pretty clear she doesn't want to see me, and besides, I don't even know which hotel she's staying at."

"You obviously care about her, a lot."

Lizzy closed her eyes and lowered her head.

"It's okay, Lizzy. It's natural."

She spun around. "No, Chris, it's not. I gave my everything to Maurice. I don't think I have it in me to love again, and Judith deserves to be loved."

"It sounds to me as if you already love her."

Lizzy opened her mouth to refute him but knew in that instant that he was right. She rubbed the back of her neck in frustration. "Christ, Chris. I never expected this. I never thought I could…" She stammered, unable to finish her sentence.

Chris stood and placed a hand on her shoulder. "What are you going to do?"

Lizzy turned to look back out the window, searching for the answer, and sighed. "I don't know."

❖

Judith couldn't sleep. She felt too overwhelmed by contradictory emotions and couldn't believe the position she'd put them in again. Things had been going so well, and somehow she'd gone and messed it all up. She'd been lucky to find a cheap hotel at such short notice, but the room was very small and Emily was thrashing about in her sleep next to her. Emily had been extremely upset about leaving Lizzy's and it tore at Judith's heart to know that her actions were causing her such distress. She felt guilty for separating them, knowing how fond they had grown of each other, and guilty for leaving the way she did.

She had no idea how Lizzy felt about what happened between them, but she knew for certain she would be hurt by the way she had left. Leaving the note had been the cowardly way and was an affront to the friendship that had grown between them, but she'd been too scared to face her. She had never expected to find herself attracted to a woman, and although the revelation that she was had taken her by surprise, it wasn't the fact that Lizzy was a woman that frightened her. It was the intensity of what she had felt that had scared her.

Lizzy's kiss had felt natural and exhilarating, and the connection she had felt with her had reached into her soul and had awoken in her a yearning she had never felt before. It compared to nothing she'd ever felt for anyone. Even when she'd first been in love with Menno, she had never felt that way when they'd kissed, and considering what had happened between her and Menno, the idea that she could feel so intensely about someone else scared the life out of her. She no longer trusted her own heart. She'd listened to it before and she'd only gotten hurt. Unsure what to do with her emotions, she'd panicked, scared of making a mistake, but even now, despite her fear and confusion, she longed to see Lizzy. She fought the urge to call her, to hear her voice, to make sure she was all right, because she needed time. Time and space to sort out her feelings and to understand what they meant.

❖

"So where's the cheap labor?"

Lizzy looked up from the script she was reading and found a very tired-looking Anita standing before her. She was sipping coffee from a large mug and offered Lizzy the other one she was holding. Everyone on set was now living on caffeine. They were in their final week of filming, and the demanding schedule was starting to take its toll on the cast and crew. Not only were they trying to keep to their deadline, but they were also trying to reshoot a few scenes they hadn't initially planned on. This was the first Wednesday afternoon that Lizzy hadn't needed to go pick up Emily from school and bring her to the studio, and she had hoped Emily's absence would go unnoticed. She accepted the coffee Anita was offering her and hoped a stupid joke would suffice.

"She found herself a better paying job."

"Cute! So, where is she?"

Lizzy frowned. "She's with her mom."

"Where's the mom?"

Lizzy had not yet told her that Judith and Emily were no longer living with her and she didn't particularly want to tell her now. She would rather pretend that the whole thing had never happened, and she couldn't do that if she had to talk about it. She tried to keep the frustration out of her voice. "What's with all the questions?"

"It's a Wednesday, and normally at this time you're rushing off to pick the little one up."

"Well, not this Wednesday." Lizzy pretended to concentrate on the script again.

Anita took another sip of her coffee and eyed Lizzy suspiciously. "Isn't that play of hers coming up soon?"

Lizzy kept staring at the script.

"If my memory serves me correctly, it's tomorrow night, isn't it? I'll bet you'll be looking forward to that."

Lizzy knew better than most just how astute Anita could be,

and she had the sinking feeling that she already knew. She slowly lifted her eyes and met Anita's penetrating gaze.

"My parents were always promising me things, Lizzy, as compensation for never being around, but they never kept their word. That hurt me more than the knowledge that they were too busy to make time for me. If you've promised the girl you'll be there, then you need to be there. Whatever happened between you and Judith, that girl is owed her promise."

Anita's words slowly fluttered their way past Lizzy's denial and settled around her already heavy heart. She didn't need Anita to remind her of the play. She'd been trying hard to put it at the back of her mind for the last few days, telling herself she had no right to be there and there was no way she could go.

Anita started to move away, but Lizzy called after her.

"How did you know?"

Anita smiled affectionately. "For the past few months there was a light behind your smile. This past week you haven't smiled once. It doesn't take a genius to it figure out."

❖

Lizzy explained to the woman who was sitting behind a children's desk just inside the school's main entrance that she was there to see Emily Hilford perform in the play but that she had lost her ticket. She didn't feel comfortable lying to the woman, especially as she seemed to be such a good soul, and if she'd believed in God she might have uttered a Hail Mary, but she didn't have a choice, because she'd never been given a ticket.

She had arrived a little late on purpose so as not to bump into Judith and was the only one left in the corridor except for the kind lady scanning a list of children's names.

"Ah, yes. Emily Hilford. Yes, two tickets were ordered and only one has been handed in tonight." The woman scribbled something behind Emily's name and with a cheerful smile gave Lizzy a stub of paper. "You've only missed a few minutes. Just go through those doors there to the left."

Lizzy thanked her as she pocketed the stub. Then she made her way quietly through the auditorium door. There was already a little boy on stage nervously introducing the story to all the parents and family members seated before him. Except for the stage, the auditorium was dark and everybody's attention seemed to be focused on the little boy, so nobody seemed to notice her entering. She decided to stay where she was, at the back of the auditorium, and she leaned against the wall, waiting for Emily to appear.

When Emily came charging onto the stage with her gang of pirates behind her, Lizzy felt an enormous sense of pride. She was acting her part so well: her sword held high, her voice clear and loud, and she had the pirate's swagger down to perfection. Lizzy watched as Emily led her pirates into battle, struggling to defeat Peter Pan. She empathized with their capture and applauded the cunningness of their escape as they headed off into the sunset, planning their next attack.

When the lights came on and the kids all walked back onstage together to take their bow, everybody rose and clapped enthusiastically, as did Lizzy. She could see Emily waving at someone in one of the front rows. She couldn't see her from where she stood, but she knew it could only be Judith. It felt strange to be so close to them both and not be seen.

The kids left the stage and the parents started making their way to the exit. Lizzy intended on leaving before the rest, but she found herself in the middle of a crowd. She was forced to patiently jostle alongside everybody else until she could slip through the auditorium doors only to find that people were lingering in the corridor, talking to one another about their kids. As politely as she could she pushed her way through them and was nearly at the exit when she heard Emily shout. *"Lizzy!"*

She turned around to see Emily, still in her pirate's costume, running toward her. Lizzy bent and caught her in her arms.

"You came. I knew you would."

"Of course I did." Lizzy hugged her back.

"Was I okay?"

Lizzy spoke with pride. "You were fantastic. Nobody could have done it better."

"Did you see the bit where I tackled Peter Pan and escaped out of his trap?"

"Yep, I saw everything." Lizzy loved the sparkle in her eyes.

"Have you seen Mommy?"

Lizzy only hesitated for a second before answering, "No, I haven't."

"Shall I go find her?".

Lizzy tapped the top of Emily's hat playfully, trying to keep it lighthearted. "No. That's okay. I'll see her another time."

Emily's face turned sullen. "Why can't we live with you anymore?"

Lizzy's heart started pounding against her chest as she tried to think of a suitable answer and wondered what Judith had already told her.

"Sometimes things don't work out the way we want them to. Your mother and I, we…we decided this was best."

Emily furrowed her eyebrows. "Do you want me to talk to her?"

Emily's innocence made Lizzy catch her breath. "No, sweetheart. Your mother and I will sort this out when the time is right." Lizzy could only hope she was telling the truth. "Now, you need to go find her before she starts worrying about where you are."

Emily wrapped her arms around Lizzy's neck and hugged her again, making it even harder for Lizzy to let her go. "Can I still come see you?"

Lizzy couldn't bring herself to say no and at the same time didn't want to make things even more difficult for Judith, but she couldn't think of anything else to say. "Maybe we can sort something out if your mommy says it's okay."

Lizzy's words brought a smile back to Emily's face and made their parting much easier.

As Lizzy walked back to the car she thought about how much her life had changed.

For more than ten years she had shared her life with a woman who had made her feel complete. Maurice's death had torn a rift through her very existence, and her world had shattered into insignificant fragments that barely mirrored past happiness and promise. She had wanted to end her own life, unable to cope with the pain, anger, and emptiness that engulfed her, but in her desperate need to give Maurice her last wish, she had continued on.

For three years she had managed to get up each morning and perform the practical necessities of life without zest. Then Judith and Emily had entered her life and somehow brought meaning back to it. Emily's playful abandon had reminded Lizzy how beautiful life could be, and watching Judith struggle to redefine herself had given her a renewed insight to a life outside of her own misery. They had inadvertently enticed her to feel again and had ultimately given her a new sense of belonging.

She'd lost Maurice and then herself, and now she felt she'd lost again.

CHAPTER TWENTY-FIVE

The school bell rang and the kids rose to their feet, eager to escape school and head into the freedom of afterschool hours.

Judith watched from behind her desk as her pupils disappeared into the school halls and realized she'd just survived her first day back at teaching again. It had been a nerve-racking experience, but as soon as she had walked into her first class of the day filled with young eager faces curiously watching her every move, she had known that she was finally back where she belonged.

The realization filled her with a thrill of achievement and her first impulse was to call Lizzy to tell her all about it. Her heart sank as she remembered that that was no longer possible.

She knew Lizzy had attended the play last week because Emily had told her. Emily was still upset about leaving Lizzy and had asked Judith every day since if they could go see her. It had made her day to know that Lizzy had come to watch her play. Judith hadn't been surprised or upset about it. A part of her had known that Lizzy would turn up, because she had never yet let Emily down. Another part of her had secretly hoped that she would, so that she would have an excuse to see her. She missed her and wanted to reach out to her, to at least put things right between them. She felt she owed her that much, but every time she picked up the phone to call her, her nerves got the better of her.

For the past two weeks she had done little else but think about

Lizzy and the way she made her feel. She had come to care for Lizzy a great deal during the past months and she had cherished the friendship that had developed between them, but somewhere along the way her feelings had grown into something more than just friendly affection. After dancing with Lizzy at Anita's party she had been aware of this change, but she had tried to ignore it. Then Lizzy had opened up to her about her past and her feelings for her had only grown stronger, but still, she had tried to ignore their meaning. When Lizzy kissed her, she inadvertently tore down Judith's fragile safety net, and Judith had felt compelled to run.

She'd only just left a long-term relationship with a man who, at one point in her life, she had been convinced was the only one for her. Then, from one day to the next, she had found herself trying to make her way in a world she no longer recognized. That was scary enough, but to admit that she was maybe falling in love again, that was downright terrifying. The initial shock of Lizzy's kiss and the intense feelings it had evoked had subsided and what remained was a longing to be with her. She now realized she had left Menno because she no longer loved him. She'd left Lizzy because she did.

Lizzy contemplated lighting up a cigarette. While Judith and Emily had been staying with her she had refrained from smoking indoors and had nearly stopped altogether, but now that she was alone again she couldn't think of a good enough reason not to light one up. She got up to hunt for a packet when the doorbell rang. It was already late and she neither expected nor wanted company. She was still deciding whether to answer it or not when the doorbell rang a second time. With a reluctant sigh she headed out into the hallway and wearily opened the door. Her heart immediately started beating faster when she saw who it was.

Judith smiled nervously. "Can I come in?"

Lizzy didn't know what to say and merely stepped back to let her in. As Judith passed her she caught a whiff of her perfume, and its scent tantalized her senses, reminding her just how much she had missed it. She closed the door and took a moment to gather herself before turning to face Judith.

"Has something happened? Is Emily okay?"

Judith answered quickly. "Yes, yes, she's fine except for the fact that she's not all that happy with me and she misses you."

Lizzy hated the idea that her actions were causing trouble between Emily and her mother. "I'm sorry I came to the play. It wasn't my intention to make things harder for you or her."

"No, no, it was good you came. It was what she wanted."

An awkward silence fell between them. Lizzy still didn't know why Judith was there so late at night and had no idea what she should do next.

"Erm, do you want something to drink?"

It seemed to take an eternity before Judith replied, and when she did it was nearly a whisper. "Emily's not the only one who misses you."

Lizzy heard the words, she definitely heard the words, but did they mean what she thought they meant, what she hoped they meant? She realized how much she longed to take Judith into her arms, to feel her close again. The thought made her skin burn. She knew she was supposed to say something, but she didn't know what. She couldn't risk telling Judith what she was thinking or what she felt. Having her so close again felt so precious that she didn't dare risk scaring her away again.

She cleared her throat and tried to sound even. "I'll make us something to drink." She started moving away.

"Lizzy, wait, please."

Lizzy felt Judith's fingertips on her arm gently making her stop.

"I'm sorry, I really am." Judith stepped closer. "I ran away from you. What happened between us…I didn't expect that from myself, I didn't expect any of it."

Lizzy could hardly breathe. "Look, Judith, that night—"

"I'm not just talking about that night. I'm talking about all of it. The way you were with Emily, the things you did for us. The way we all were with each other. You were so kind and understanding. I don't know when it started, but I started looking forward to seeing you and missed you when I didn't. I enjoyed telling you about my day, wanting to hear about yours, and the more I learned about you, the more I wanted to know. You intrigued me and inspired me. You gave me the feeling it was all right to be me. Lizzy, the moment I left Menno I started a voyage of self-discovery, and you've been there with me every step of the way."

Lizzy couldn't believe what she was hearing, and a swarm of emotions swept through her thundering heart.

Judith took a step toward her. "I never wanted to hurt you, Lizzy, but I needed time to get my head around what I was feeling, to put things back into perspective, to realize what it is I want."

Lizzy's mouth felt so dry it was difficult to speak and she couldn't look Judith in the eye. "What do you want?"

Judith took yet another step closer and with a trembling hand reached up and gently turned Lizzy's face toward her. "You, us, in whatever form that takes."

Before Lizzy could say or think or do anything, Judith leaned in and gently kissed her. Their lips barely touched, but it fueled the pent-up fire that had been ignited by their previous kiss, and Lizzy could no longer hold back. She wrapped her arm around Judith's waist, pulling her in, and kissed her passionately.

Judith felt a surging heat as Lizzy's passion engulfed her and all thought vanished. She was aware of Lizzy's hand under her coat pulling the back of her blouse free from her pants and then felt her lungs constrict as warm hands caressed her skin. She broke free from the kiss, gasping for air. She looked into Lizzy's eyes and saw that same intense look she had seen that night they had first kissed, but now it was even more breathtaking. Judith had never felt so wanted. She clasped Lizzy's hand and on trembling legs led her down the hall to her old bedroom.

The curtains had not been drawn and the light of the moon filled the room, outlining the contour of the bed. Judith felt unsure, but

Lizzy stepped forward and gently slid Judith's coat off her shoulders before turning her so that her back was against the wall. She held Judith's wrists down at her sides and kissed her slowly around her neck, along her collarbone and down to the crest of her breasts. The tenderness of Lizzy's kisses created tingling flutters at the spot where her lips touched her skin, and the simultaneous feeling of Lizzy's anchoring grip on her wrists only enhanced the sensation.

Then Lizzy's hands started a soft trail up her arms and down her sides, ever so lightly caressing the sides of her breasts. Judith moved slightly, wanting more contact, but Lizzy's hands continued their journey down and across her stomach, where they pulled the rest of her blouse free before slowly undoing each button. As the blouse fell away, Lizzy kissed the newly exposed skin of her shoulders, causing warm waves to ripple throughout the rest of her body. She tried to turn Lizzy's face toward her, needing to feel Lizzy's mouth on hers again, but at that same moment, Lizzy trailed her hands up along her back, massaging the muscles along the way. Judith's head snapped back as an involuntary moan forced its way past her lips. Then Lizzy unclasped her bra. The sensation of her bra falling away made her want to hold Lizzy even closer to her, but Lizzy leaned back and caressed her breasts with her eyes. Judith felt terribly vulnerable, but then Lizzy whispered in a tone she didn't recognize. "God, you're beautiful."

Lizzy's words sent a bolt of sensations ricocheting through her body, settling between her legs. Judith didn't think she could stand up much longer, but before she could think another thought, Lizzy was kissing her again, long and deep. She felt herself falling into her as she started to shake. Her body screamed for release, but it was too much, too soon. She clasped Lizzy's hands, stilling them, and rested her head on her shoulder as she tried to catch her breath. Lizzy seemed to understand and gently embraced her and simply held her. Judith could feel Lizzy's heart beating against her chest and concentrated on its mesmerizing rhythm as she let the burning throbbing of her body simmer down to a mere hum.

The warmth of their embrace felt like a cocoon, and in it the spirit of time stood still. Judith had never felt such serenity. She remembered when they had danced and how she had felt the urge to kiss Lizzy's neck. Smiling, she turned her head and very softly kissed the side of Lizzy's neck. To her exquisite delight, she heard and felt Lizzy's sharp intake of breath and wanted to feel more of her. She started to lift Lizzy's shirt, inviting Lizzy to raise her arms in compliance. As soon as the shirt was over her head, Lizzy leaned forward and kissed her again, with excruciating tenderness. The softness of Lizzy's lips immediately caused the fire simmering inside her to flare, and she kissed Lizzy back with a passion she had never felt before. She felt Lizzy moan into her mouth and somewhere through her consciousness was aware that they were moving. Lizzy's embrace tightened and Judith was guided down onto the bed. Lizzy's passion was the mirror to her own and Judith held her tightly, pulling her down on top of her. Suddenly feeling Lizzy's thigh between her own sent a jolt of lightning up her spine, and she was momentarily blinded by invisible white snowflakes. She couldn't tell if Lizzy was moving up against her or if she was moving up against Lizzy, but it didn't matter and she didn't care. Her body demanded its release and when she felt Lizzy's lips on her neck again, it came in long thundering waves and she fell into a blissful peace.

❖

Judith's body hummed with contentedness as she reveled in the warmth and the delicate scent of Lizzy's body next to her. She could tell by her soft breathing that she was asleep and marveled at the intimacy of such a gentle sound.

The honesty of Lizzy's passion had been breathtaking, but the intensity of her own desire had been astounding. Every fiber of her being had craved Lizzy, and the oneness she had felt with her had awoken within her an emboldened sense of self. She'd been afraid to accept the love she felt for Lizzy, scared of getting hurt, but finding the courage to face her fear had brought her even closer to Lizzy.

She felt a slight chill on her partially exposed back and lazily opened her eyes. The darkness of night had surrendered to the dawn, and the early morning rays of sunlight gracefully showered them with splendor. She realized that Lizzy's arm was draped across her stomach, and the simple gesture made her heart swell with a heightened spirit of belonging. She had no idea where they would go from here, but in her heart, she knew that whatever path she took with Lizzy, it would always lead her home.

Mindful not to wake her, she reached for the folded blanket at the foot of the bed and carefully pulled it up over them before snuggling back into Lizzy's embrace.

Epilogue

Lizzy drove along Plantage Middenlaan, past the university's botanical garden toward Artis Zoo. It was Emily's birthday and she had chosen a visit to the zoo as her special treat.

That morning Judith and Lizzy had been awoken by Emily jumping up and down on their bed squealing her delight at her presents, offering them a deluge of hugs of gratitude. Lizzy hadn't wanted to leave them, but she'd had to go to work for a few hours so had arranged to meet them at the zoo gate. She was running a little late and waited impatiently at the traffic lights.

She couldn't believe how happy she felt. She still missed Maurice, but having Judith and Emily in her life had erased the vast hole Maurice's death had left, and their love had helped her breach the rift of her grief. In her heart she believed Maurice's spirit still lived on and chose to believe her goodness was shining down in places it otherwise could never have reached. Maurice would always own a piece of her heart, but Lizzy was now free to enjoy the memory of her without the onslaught of pain, and was finally able to fulfill her promise to her. She had never thought it possible to love again, but Judith had woven a tapestry of light around her heart and Lizzy loved her with all that she was.

She turned off onto Plantage Kerklaan and spotted Judith and Emily waiting in the queue. They were happily chatting to one another, and just seeing them fueled the love Lizzy felt for them. She quickly parked the car and crossed the road to join them.

About the Author

Lindsey Stone was born in the West Midlands of England, but at the age of thirteen emigrated to the Netherlands with her mother and brother. Although she often misses the British landscape and its traditional food, she is pleased to live in a country where sexual orientation is no longer grounds for discrimination and where homosexual couples and their rights are recognized and protected by the law.

Her mind is a bustling playground filled with images, scenes, characters, and plots, all demanding her attention, but in those moments when they are kind enough to give her some peace, she can be found playing her guitar, or building something out in the garage, or simply slouched on the couch next to her trusted shadow, her Malinois dog, who somehow always seems to get the most space.

Books Available From Bold Strokes Books

The Midnight Hunt by L.L. Raand. Medic Drake McKennan takes a chance and loses, and her life will never be the same—because when she wakes up after surviving a life-threatening illness, she is no longer human. (978-1-60282-140-8)

Long Shot by D. Jackson Leigh. Love isn't safe, which is exactly why equine veterinarian Tory Greyson wants no part of it—until Leah Montgomery and a horse that won't give up convince her otherwise. (978-1-60282-141-5)

In Medias Res by Yolanda Wallace. Sydney has forgotten her entire life, and the one woman who holds the key to her memory, and her heart, doesn't want to be found. (978-1-60282-142-2)

Awakening to Sunlight by Lindsey Stone. Neither Judith or Lizzy is looking for companionship, and certainly not love—but when their lives become entangled, they discover both. (978-1-60282-143-9)

Fever by VK Powell. Hired gun Zakaria Chambers is hired to provide a simple escort service to philanthropist Sara Ambrosini, but nothing is as simple as it seems, especially love. (978-1-60282-135-4)

High Risk by JLee Meyer. Can actress Kate Hoffman really risk all she's worked for to take a chance on love? Or is it already too late? (978-1-60282-136-1)

Missing Lynx by Kim Baldwin and Xenia Alexiou. On the trail of a notorious serial killer, Elite Operative Lynx's growing attraction to a mysterious mercenary could be her path to love—or to death. (978-1-60282-137-8)

Spanking New by Clifford Henderson. A poignant, hilarious, unforgettable look at life, love, gender, and the essence of what makes us who we are. (978-1-60282-138-5)

Magic of the Heart by C.J. Harte. CEO Susan Hettinger and wild, impulsive rock star M.J. Carson couldn't be more different if they tried—but opposites attract in ways neither woman can resist. (978-1-60282-131-6)

Ambereye by Gill McKnight. Jolie Garoul is falling in love with her assistant. The big problem is, Jolie is a werewolf. (978-1-60282-132-3)

Collision Course by C.P. Rowlands. Tragedy leaves Brie O'Malley and Jordan Carter fearful and alone. Can they find the courage to take a second chance on love? (978-1-60282-133-0)

Mephisto Aria by Justine Saracen. Opera singer Katherina Marov's destiny may be to repeat the mistakes of her father when she becomes involved in a dangerous love affair. (978-1-60282-134-7)

Battle Scars by Meghan O'Brien. Returning Iraq war veteran Ray McKenna struggles with the battle scars that can only be healed by love. (978-1-60282-129-3)

Chaps by Jove Belle. Eden Metcalf wants nothing more than to flee from her troubled past and travel the open road—until she runs into rancher Brandi Cornwell. (978-1-60282-127-9)

Lightbearer by John Caruso. Lucifer dares to question the premise of creation itself and reveals that sin may be all that stands between us and living hell. (978-1-60282-130-9)

The Seeker by Ronica Black. FBI profiler Kennedy Scott battles ghosts from her past, deadly obsession, and the evil that haunts her. (978-1-60282-128-6)

Power Play by Julie Cannon. Businesswomen Tate Monroe and Victoria Sosa are at odds in the boardroom, but not in the bedroom. (978-1-60282-125-5)

The Remarkable Journey of Miss Tranby Quirke by Elizabeth Ridley. When love enters Tranby's life in the form of a beautiful nineteen-year-old student, Lysette McDonald, she embarks on the most remarkable journey of all. (978-1-60282-126-2)

Returning Tides by Radclyffe. Insurance investigator Ashley Walker faces more than a dangerous opponent when she returns to the town, and the woman, she left behind. (978-1-60282-123-1)

Veritas by Anne Laughlin. When the hallowed halls of academia become the stage for murder, newly appointed Dean Beth Ellis's search for the truth leads her to unexpected discoveries about her own heart. (978-1-60282-124-8)

The Pleasure Planner by Larkin Rose. Pleasure purveyor Bree Hendricks treats love like a commodity until Logan Delaney makes Bree the client in her own game. (978-1-60282-121-7)

everafter by Nell Stark and Trinity Tam. Valentine Darrow is bitten by a vampire on her way to propose to her lover Alexa Newland, and their lives and love are placed in mortal jeopardy. (978-1-60282-119-4)

Summer Winds by Andrews & Austin. When Maggie Turner hires a ranch hand to help work her thousand acres, she never expects to be attracted to the very young, very female Cash Tate. (978-1-60282-120-0)

Beggar of Love by Lee Lynch. Jefferson is the lover every woman wants to be—or to have. A revealing saga of lesbian sexuality. (978-1-60282-122-4)

The Seduction of Moxie by Colette Moody. When 1930s Broadway actress Violet London meets speakeasy singer Moxie Valette, she is instantly attracted and her Hollywood trip takes an unexpected turn. (978-1-60282-114-9)

Goldenseal by Gill McKnight. When Amy Fortune returns to her childhood home, she discovers something sinister in the air—but is former lover Leone Garoul stalking her or protecting her? (978-1-60282-115-6)

Romantic Interludes 2: Secrets edited by Radclyffe and Stacia Seaman. An anthology of sensual lesbian love stories: passion, surprises, and secret desires. (978-1-60282-116-3)

Femme Noir by Clara Nipper. Nora Delaney meets her match in Max Abbott, a sex-crazed dame who may or may not have the information Nora needs to solve a murder—but can she contain her lust for Max long enough to find out? (978-1-60282-117-0)

The Reluctant Daughter by Lesléa Newman. Heartwarming, heartbreaking, and ultimately triumphant—the story every daughter recognizes of the lifelong struggle for our mothers to really see us. (978-1-60282-118-7)

Erosistible by Gill McKnight. When Win Martin arrives at a luxurious Greek hotel for a much-anticipated week of sun and sex with her new girlfriend, she is stunned to find her ex-girlfriend, Benny, is the proprietor. Aeros Ebook. (978-1-60282-134-7)

Looking Glass Lives by Felice Picano. Cousins Roger and Alistair become lifelong friends and discover their sexuality amidst the backdrop of twentieth-century gay culture. (978-1-60282-089-0)

Breaking the Ice by Kim Baldwin. Nothing is easy about life above the Arctic Circle—except, perhaps, falling in love. At least that's what pilot Bryson Faulkner hopes when she meets Karla Edwards. (978-1-60282-087-6)

It Should Be a Crime by Carsen Taite. Two women fulfill their mutual desire with a night of passion, neither expecting more until law professor Morgan Bradley and student Parker Casey meet again…in the classroom. (978-1-60282-086-9)

Rough Trade edited by Todd Gregory. Top male erotica writers pen their own hot, sexy versions of the term "rough trade," producing some of the hottest, nastiest, and most dangerous fiction ever published. (978-1-60282-092-0)

The High Priest and the Idol by Jane Fletcher. Jemeryl and Tevi's relationship is put to the test when the Guardian sends Jemeryl on a mission that puts her not only in harm's way, but back into the sights of a previous lover. (978-1-60282-085-2)

Point of Ignition by Erin Dutton. Amid a blaze that threatens to consume them both, firefighter Kate Chambers and property owner Alexi Clark redefine love and trust. (978-1-60282-084-5)

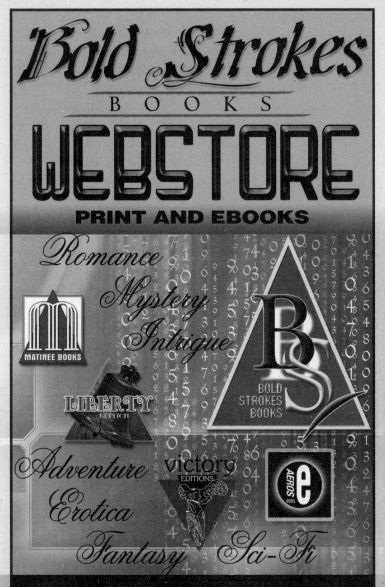